T0209169

SAVED FOR BEN:

BEN AND WANDA

JACQUELYN B. SMITH

WESTBOW
PRESS®
A DIVISION OF THOMAS NELSON
& ZONDERVAN

This is a work of fiction. All of the characters, names, incidents,
organizations, and dialogue in this novel are either the products
of the author's imagination or are used fictitiously.

WestBow Press books may be ordered through booksellers or by contacting:

WestBow Press
A Division of Thomas Nelson & Zondervan
1663 Liberty Drive
Bloomington, IN 47403
www.westbowpress.com
844-714-3454

Because of the dynamic nature of the Internet, any web addresses or
links contained in this book may have changed since publication and
may no longer be valid. The views expressed in this work are solely those
of the author and do not necessarily reflect the views of the publisher,
and the publisher hereby disclaims any responsibility for them.

Any people depicted in stock imagery provided by Getty Images are
models, and such images are being used for illustrative purposes only.
Certain stock imagery © Getty Images.

ISBN: 978-1-6642-6893-7 (sc)
ISBN: 978-1-6642-6895-1 (hc)
ISBN: 978-1-6642-6894-4 (e)

Library of Congress Control Number: 2022911126

Print information available on the last page.

WestBow Press rev. date: 7/27/2022

This *Saved for Ben* series is dedicated to my loving and nurturing grandmother, Ora Lee Woods; a second to none mother, Lillie Mae Wood; and my village. My grandmother and mother used every opportunity available to broaden my horizons and instill life changing godly principles in me.

God has connected wonderful people to my journey of spiritual growth. My village consists of those who have prayed, encouraged, and helped me during my journey of academic years, military service, and personal growth whether in Georgia, Virginia, Texas, or Florida. I am forever grateful for their love, support, and endearing friendship. Last but now least, to my son, Jeremy, a precious gift of God, who has inspired me to continue making a difference through writing for those who are willing to trust God.

CONTENTS

1

THE FIRST DATE

Wanda had agreed to go out with Ben on Friday and Saturday night. He was elated. He just needed to come up with something fun yet memorable to do. There was a carnival in a nearby town about twenty-five miles away. He did not want to drive the hour and a half back to Macon for entertainment. Finally, he decided that they would go bowling on Friday night and on Saturday, they would go to the carnival.

On Wednesday morning, Ben had a meeting with the Certified Public Accountant, Timothy Stevens. His meeting with the lawyer, Hank Jennings, had been overwhelming, when he found out all the things that his grandfather had left him. During the meeting Mr. Stevens took his time to explain all of the different accounts and what they were used for.

Ben said, "As you know I have plans to renovate the building next to the golf shop. Is there money available for the renovation?"

Timothy said excitedly, "Yes, there is. Your grandfather set up an account for it already. If we need more, we can transfer money from other accounts."

Ben said, "I should have known. Grandpa thought of everything."

Timothy agreed, "He was constantly thinking of what you would need and making sure it was set aside."

Ben asked, "How do you and Mr. Jennings get paid? Is it every time I come to you for help or advice?"

Pointing at a ledger, Timothy said, "No, we have a monthly fee which is charged to this account. This allows us to help you anytime you need it. Your Grandpa agreed upon this fee before he died. We are happy to serve you."

Ben said, "I appreciate it. I just wanted to make sure you were being compensated."

Timothy said, "I look forward to working with you. I am excited about the expansion. I tried to get your grandfather to consider renovating some of the old buildings in the city that he owned."

Ben asked, "Did he not think it was a good idea?"

Timothy said, "No, he thought it was a great idea. He just felt he was too old to take it on. When he came to me with the idea of the event center, I was surprised. We had bought that land a long time ago. I was excited to see him pursue the project."

Ben said, "I have been thinking about some of the old buildings. There really is nowhere for people to go for entertainment in Fairville. The movie theater closed down about ten years ago."

Timothy said, "You are right. Your grandfather also created another account for you. This account is for when you wanted to start some businesses. There is more than enough in there if you want to do something."

Ben said, "Again, I should not be surprised. I do want to do something. I would like to open a bowling alley, Putt-Putt golf course, and a movie theater. I think they can be very lucrative."

Timothy asked, "That's a great idea. However, do you understand that we would have to do it under the company name of C&D Enterprises?"

Ben said, "I understand. What does C&D stand for?"

Timothy said, "As you know your grandfather's first name was Charlie. His wife's name was Doris. That's where we get the C&D, Charlie and Doris. However, before he died, he told me that he wanted it to reflect Cason and Davis. Mr. Jennings changed all of the paper work to denote Cason and Davis. However, on all documents it says C&D Enterprises."

Ben wiped the tears from his eyes and said, "I can't believe he did that."

Timothy said, "He loved you very much."

After getting himself together, Ben said slowly, "I was thinking we could use some of the vacant land on Highway 15."

Timothy said, "That would be a great site for a bowling alley and an updated movie theater. The movie theater in town is old. It is too small for the cinema-plexes they have today."

Ben asked, "What do I have to do to get it started?"

Timothy said, "I will get with Hank and we will develop a plan for you to review."

Ben asked, "In the plan can we do something with the old movie theater? It looks bad."

Timothy said, "Yes, we can. We may have to tear it down. I think it is too old to bring up to code anyway."

Ben said, "I am concerned that after we build it. How will we manage it?"

Timothy said, "That is a valid concern. We will have to hire someone to manage it."

Ben said, "I don't want people to steal from me."

Timothy said, "You're right. That is the last thing, we want.

We will set up weekly audits and processes which have checks and balances. Don't worry this is done all of the time."

Ben said, "That's good to know. I am trying to build Grandpa's legacy, not lose it."

Looking at his calendar Timothy laughed and said, "You have some great ideas. Let's meet again in two weeks. I know you are also meeting with Hank, so on the alternate weeks, let's meet at eight o'clock in the morning on Wednesdays. Is it OK with you?"

Ben said, "That would be fine."

Timothy said, "Of course, my goal is to make you aware of all of your accounts and what they are used for, and how we can grow this portfolio. Do you know what everything is worth?"

Ben said, "Yes, Mr. Jennings told me approximately thirty-three million dollars."

Timothy said, "Close! It is a little over thirty-five million dollars. You are a very rich man."

Ben said, "This is all so hard to believe. I did not know Grandpa had this much money. I thought he only owned the golf shop."

Timothy said, "No one in Fairville knew. Did Hank explain to you why we have to keep this a secret?"

Ben said, "I understand that it is for my protection. Things have changed in Fairville, but this town is still not ready for a twenty-year-old, black millionaire."

Timothy laughed and said, "True! Your grandfather was white and eighty-six. Fairville was not ready for him to be a millionaire."

Ben laughed.

Timothy said, "Of course, everyone knew he owned the golf shop, but that is all they knew. Did Hank explain to you about the different accounts?"

Ben said, "Yes, he broke it down into residential rental property, commercial rental property, industrial rental property, various stocks, the golf shop, and the event center. Oh, and he also said that there was about one hundred acres of vacant land throughout the county."

Timothy said, "Correct! Over the next few weeks I will explain to you in detail about each of those categories."

Ben said, "Thank you. I would also like to donate to my church, New Providence Baptist Church."

Timothy said, "No problem! Your grandfather made charitable donations every year. No donation has been made so far this year. Usually he would make at least three a year."

Ben asked, "Did he have a certain amount that he donated?"

Timothy said, "It would range between twenty thousand and twenty-five thousand dollars to each organization."

Ben said, "Since no donations have been made so far, I would like to make a seventy-five-thousand-dollar donation to the church."

Timothy said, "I will take care of it. Remember, they will not know that it is from you."

Ben said, "I understand. I don't want them to. I have one more question. How do I access Grandpa's personal account? Mr. Jennings told me that it was now mine."

Looking at a document Timothy said, "Thank you for reminding me. Here are some checks, your balance in the personal account is exactly $259,345. I also applied for two credit cards for you. This is an American Express Black card. There is no limit. This is a VISA credit card, there is a limit of ten thousand dollars. I will just pay it off for you at the end of each month."

Ben said, "Wow, credit cards! How do we pay off these bills? Will it come from my personal account?"

Timothy smiled and said, "No, your grandfather set up another account for any personal bills you may have. This is the account that we used for the vehicles or anything else he needed."

Ben asked, "How much money is in that account?"

Timothy smiled and said, "Approximately five-hundred thousand dollars. This account is set up to receive one percent profit from each of the businesses. So, at the end of the year, money is transferred into this account. It did not start out this high, but each year funds are transferred to it. However, more funds have been transferred there since the golf shop has been doing so well. It also receives money from the real estate accounts. Your grandfather rarely used it."

Ben said, "I don't know what to say. I am trying my best not to feel overwhelmed again."

Timothy said, "I understand. Over the next few weeks, you will get a better understanding. I heard that you are pursuing your master's degree."

Ben said, "Yes, I am. I will be taking classes part-time. I know it will take me longer, but with everything going on. That is all I can do."

Timothy said, "Before you know it, it will be over."

Ben asked, "What about a salary for my mom for managing the event center?"

Timothy said, "Your Grandpa already set up the event center account. There is money there for salaries and an operational budget. I am sure the event center will turn a profit very quickly. I am so glad your grandfather built the event center, we needed it here in Fairville."

Ben asked, "Do you have an idea of what the salary should be for the manager?"

Timothy said, "Yes, I do. Your grandfather had me research

it. The average salary in 1978 for an event center manager is twenty-five thousand dollars a year."

Ben said, "Twenty-five thousand dollars a year! That is substantially more than my mom made at the textile factory."

Timothy said, "You're right. We expect the event center to bring in at least fifty thousand dollars the first year and more each following year. Your mother is going to be busy. Based on our projections, the rooms should be booked at least three days a week. During the summer, I am sure it will be booked five days a week."

Ben said, "That is great. The center is packed with everything we need. However, if needed, how would Mom order things?"

Timothy said, "I have a budget set aside for utilities, insurance, and everything else. This outlines exactly what has to be paid each month. It also has a budget for her to operate under. I have a credit card for her to order anything she needs. Those expenses will be paid out of the account each month."

Ben said, "Wow! Money does make things much easier."

Timothy smiled and said, "Yes, it does."

Ben asked, "Is there a health insurance plan for employees of C&D Enterprises?"

Timothy said, "Yes there is. Your grandfather set up a plan about thirty years ago. Your grandfather had some health issues. The health insurance plan is still open, so we will add you and your mother."

Ben asked, "The health benefit is only for full-time employees correct?"

Timothy said, "Yes. I will have insurance cards for you when you come back to our next meeting."

Ben asked, "Suppose I got married, would my family be covered under the plan?"

Timothy said, "Yes, they would. Mr. Cason's wife was covered under a similar plan before she died. Since your brother and sister are dependents of your mother, they are eligible for coverage too."

Ben said, "That's good to know. Is it affordable?"

Timothy passed Ben the checks and credit card and said, "Yes, the rates are very affordable. I will contact your mother to schedule a time for her to complete the necessary forms."

Ben stood up and said, "Thank you for being so patient with me."

Timothy said, "I look forward to working with you. I knew your grandfather about twenty-five years. The last six years of his life were the happiest that I have ever seen him. You could see the difference, when he moved in with your family. He loved you all very much."

Ben said, "We loved him very much too."

Timothy said, "I heard a lot of people in town talking about him moving in with your family. Some did not understand it."

Ben said, "I am sure they didn't."

Timothy said, "I was able to witness the love he had for you and the love your family showed him. It was amazing."

Ben said, "I am going to miss him. Thank you, Mr. Stevens."

Ben stood up, shook his hand, and left. When Ben arrived back at the golf shop, Wanda was cleaning the restroom.

Ben said, "Good morning Beautiful!"

Wanda smiled and said, "I'm sure I look a mess. It seems like each day, we get more and more customers. I have only been open for thirty minutes and I have checked out ten people. One man was waiting at the door for me to unlock it!"

Ben laughed and said, "People have heard about you and want to see for themselves."

Wanda laughed and said, "That is fine, as long as they buy something too."

Ben smiled and said, "I have some ideas for our dates this weekend?"

Wanda said excitedly, "Great, what are we doing?"

Ben said, "On Friday night, let's go bowling over in Bridgetown. Then on Saturday, there is a carnival in Harrisburg. Both of those cities are about twenty-five minutes away."

Wanda said, "Sounds great, I love bowling. You won't be upset if I beat you, will you?"

Ben said, "I should be asking you the same thing. My college roommate, Caleb, and I bowled regularly in Macon. So, don't expect me to feel sorry for you."

Wanda laughed and said, "I accept the challenge. May the best bowler win."

Ben smiled and said, "I do have a competitive spirit; so, I don't want you to cry when I beat you."

Wanda said, "I won't. I can accept defeat. The question is can you."

Ben laughed and hugged Wanda. They worked hard the rest of the day. Ben washed the vehicles in the back. He washed the van, his truck, and Wanda's car. He wanted to make sure his truck was ready for their date. Wanda washed the windows in the front between customers. She mopped and waxed the floor, she then dusted the display cases. She also drafted a letter to be mailed to the customers.

The rest of the week flew by. Ben finished the letter. He took the letter to Mr. Jennings' secretary with a copy of the mailing list. He explained what he needed. She said that she would take care of it. He also picked up Wanda's pay check from Mr. Steven's office.

It was finally Friday night. Ben picked up Wanda from her

Uncle Robert's house at seven o'clock. When she walked out of the door, she looked beautiful.

Ben said, "Wanda, you look beautiful. I hate that we are just going bowling."

Wanda said, "Thank you. I'm only wearing some jeans and a red shirt."

Ben said, "It's a simple outfit, but you look beautiful in it."

Wanda smiled and said, "Thanks. I also wanted to thank you for washing and detailing my car. It has never been detailed like that."

Ben said, "I enjoyed cleaning it for you."

Wanda said, "Ben, don't start something, you can't keep up."

Ben smiled and said, "I won't!"

Wanda said, "If you want to back out of our competition, you still have time."

Ben exclaimed, "I don't care how beautiful you are. I plan to beat you bowling tonight."

Wanda smiled and said, "I was thinking we could bowl three games. I think you can win at least one."

Ben laughed and said, "That would be fine."

They arrived at the bowling alley. Surprisingly for a Friday night it was not crowded.

After they got shoes and found balls Ben asked, "Would you like something to eat or drink?"

Wanda said, "Yes, I would like a cheeseburger, fries, and a coke!"

Ben said, "Oh, you're a coke girl!"

Wanda said, "Yes, that's one of my vices."

Ben returned with the food.

After they ate, Wanda said, "Are you ready? There's still time for you to change your mind."

Ben laughed and said, "You really think you're going to win."

They bowled the first game. Ben won. Wanda said nothing. Wanda won the second game, 130 to his 120.

Ben said, "Oh! I didn't expect you to make that last strike."

Wanda said, "I just needed to warm up."

Ben tried his best, but Wanda won the third game 170-145.

Ben said, "I didn't expect you to be able to bowl this well. You trounced me."

Wanda smiled and said, "Don't ever underestimate me!"

Ben hugged her and laughed.

Wanda said, "Let's take a picture!"

Wanda pulled out her camera and the people who were bowling next to them, were kind enough to take a picture. On Saturday, they worked hard at the shop.

Wanda said, "I'm excited about our date tonight. I haven't been to a carnival in a long time."

Ben said, "Caleb and I would go to the Georgia State Fair in Macon during the month of October. Maybe we can go this year."

Wanda said, "I would like that."

A customer walked in. It was Jerry Green.

Ben said, "Good Morning Mr. Green. This is my assistant, Wanda. Wanda, this is Mr. Green."

Jerry Green said, "It is nice to meet you Wanda. Ben, how is construction coming?"

Ben said, "It is going well."

Jerry Green asked, "Do you have any of those yellow tees I like?"

Ben said, "Yes sir, I try to keep them in stock for you."

Wanda said, "I will get them!"

Ben said, "Thank you. Mr. Green, I have some work in

the back. Wanda will take good care of you. It is always nice
to see you."

Jerry Green said, "You too!"

Wanda returned and asked, "Mr. Green, how many tees
would you like?"

Jerry Green said, "About twenty-four would be fine."

Wanda asked, "Do you need anything else?"

Jerry Green said, "Not today."

Wanda asked, "Why do you like these yellows tees?"

Jerry Green replied, "I am color blind, but I can see these
yellow tees better than the white."

Wanda suggested, "We have some yellow gloves that you
might like!"

Jerry Green said, "Really, let me see them."

Wanda retrieved the gloves and said "I figured you wore
an extra-large. Try these on."

Jerry Green said, "I like them. The other gloves I have are
black. I like these better."

Wanda asked, "Would you like to take them home today?"

Jerry Green said, "Yes, I would."

Wanda said, "We also have some yellow balls. They are
new. I am not sure you would like that shade of yellow."

Jerry Green said excitedly, "Let me see them!"

Wanda retrieved the yellow balls and said, "We only have
two boxes left."

Jerry Green said, "I will take both boxes."

Wanda smiled and said, "I am glad we had some things
you could use."

Jerry Green paid for his merchandise and said, "I am glad
too. I will see you soon."

When Mr. Green left, Ben rushed back into the front of

the store and exclaimed, "Wanda, I can't believe that you sold all those things!"

Wanda smiled.

Ben said, "We have cases of those yellow balls."

Wanda said, "I know! I wanted him to think we only had those left!"

Ben exclaimed, "So he would buy both boxes!"

Wanda laughed and said, "It's all in how you present things to the customer. You want them to think they are getting a good deal and something that no one else has."

Ben hugged Wanda and said, "You're amazing. Thanks for the lesson!"

The rest of the day went by fast. Ben picked Wanda up at seven o'clock.

He opened the passenger door of the truck and said, "Wanda, even though I have been with you all day. Yet, you somehow manage to look more beautiful each time I pick you up."

Wanda said, "Thanks! You look very nice too. I love the cologne you're wearing."

Ben said, "I'm glad."

Wanda said, "I won't challenge you to anything tonight. I don't want you to feel bad."

Ben laughed and said, "No problem. If I see something that I can beat you at, don't worry I will challenge you!"

Wanda said, "That's fine, but be careful."

Ben laughed.

They had a wonderful time at the carnival. It was a beautiful, summer night about eighty-five degrees with a zephyr. They laughed at everything. They tried deep-fried Oreos. They both agreed that they were delicious. They rode on the roller coaster, the Ferris Wheel, and the swings. They posed for a caricature. They had a great time and took a lot of pictures.

When the night was over, Wanda said, "Ben, I had a great time tonight."

Ben said, "I did too. I know there are only two more weeks before classes start at the university and you will be going back to Macon. Would you consider dating me exclusively?"

Wanda asked, "Are you asking me to be your girlfriend?"

Ben smiled and said, "Yes, I am!"

Wanda said, "I would love to be."

Ben asked, "Is it too much for you to see me at work and date me too?"

Wanda said, "No, not at all. I like spending time with you."

Ben said, "I enjoy spending time with you too."

Ben leaned over and kissed her on her cheek.

Wanda smiled.

The next two weeks flew by. Ben and Wanda went on a date every Friday and Saturday night. They attended church together and after work, they had Sunday dinner at his mom's house. His brother, David, cooked something delicious each Sunday.

It was now the second week in August. David picked up Mary, their sister, from her two-week camp in Athens. She had a great time. She loved the University of Georgia's campus. That's where she wanted to go to college. David left for the Atlanta Institute of Art on the following Sunday. Everyone was sad. He promised to be home sometime in October.

Wanda planned to leave on the following Thursday, she wanted to spend her last weekend of the summer at home with her parents.

While at work on Thursday, Wanda said, "I talked to my mom last night. I received a letter from the federal grant people.

It denoted the amount of federal aid I would receive this year. It's lower than the amount I usually get. My mom started working again last year, so my family income is higher."

Ben asked, "Do you use the federal grant to cover your tuition?"

Wanda said, "No, I have a scholarship for my tuition. I use the grant money to cover my housing and meals. I will figure something out."

Ben asked, "Are you sure?"

Wanda said, "Yes! I plan to leave this afternoon around four o'clock to drive home. I will miss you."

Ben said, "I will miss you too. Are we on for lunch on Monday after my second class?"

Wanda said, "Yes, I'll meet you outside of the student union around one o'clock!"

When Wanda drove away, Ben was very sad. He picked up the phone and called Dean Smith, the head of the Business College at Middle Georgia State University.

Dean Smith asked, "How is my favorite business graduate?"

Ben said, "I am doing well sir."

Dean Smith asked, "What can I do for you?"

Ben said, "I know that I am on scholarship for my graduate classes. I have some money and I don't need the scholarship anymore."

Dean Smith said, "Ben, you earned that scholarship. I don't want you to give it up."

Ben asked, "OK, thank you! Can I donate and you start a new scholarship?"

Dean Smith said, "That would be great."

Ben asked, "I would like the scholarship to be for senior business students. Could you check to see if Wanda Knowlton would qualify?"

Dean Smith said, "Of course, I can. Would you like for this to be a recurring scholarship or just a one time?"

Ben said, "Recurring. I will drop off a check to you early Monday morning."

Dean Smith said, "I look forward to seeing you again. Goodbye."

Ben hung up the phone. Closed the shop and called his accountant, Timothy Stevens.

2

THE ARGUMENT

It was Monday, the first day of college classes. Wanda was scheduled to meet Ben for lunch. Ben happily waited at their designated spot. When Ben saw Wanda walking toward him, he stood up with a big smile on his face. He noticed that Wanda was not smiling. When he tried to hug her, she pushed him away and stepped back.

Ben asked, "Wanda, what's wrong?"

Wanda asked angrily, "Did you create a scholarship and tell Dean Smith to give it to me?"

Ben said, "Uh!"

Wanda said firmly, "Don't lie Ben, you're not good at it!"

Ben said, "You're right. I'm not good at lying. I did donate to the university and asked them to establish a scholarship. I did not tell Dean Smith to give it to you. I did ask him to look to see if you were eligible."

Wanda said sternly, "You knew that I was eligible. That's why you created the scholarship. Is that correct?"

Ben said, "That is true?"

Wanda said, "I am not a damsel in distress, I don't need you to be my knight in shiny armor. I am a strong woman, capable of taking care of herself. I know how to problem solve."

Ben tried to interject.

Wanda exclaimed, "You did not trust me to get it done myself. I could have had a Plan B, C, and D. You didn't know. You didn't ask. You knew that I would not accept the money from you, so you went behind my back to deceive me. That's why I'm mad. Mad isn't the word. I am hurt. I am hurt that you did not trust or believe in me. I don't love you for your money and you don't have to save me!"

Ben said, "I only wanted to help you. I was not trying to deceive you."

Wanda said loudly, "What do you call creating a scholarship just for me behind my back. When were you going to tell me the truth? Ever! No, you probably were not. You were just going to let me believe that I earned the scholarship."

Ben pleaded, "Wanda, please try to understand my motives!"

Still angry Wanda said, "Your motives may have been noble, but the results are the same. You did not trust me, believe in me, and you tried to deceive me. That makes me think, if you did it once, you will do it again. Can I trust you?"

Ben said loudly, "Of course, you can trust me Wanda. I just had not thought about it like that."

Wanda said sternly, "I had a plan to get the money. I am very upset with you for not believing in me. I do not want to have lunch with you."

Wanda turned around and walked away briskly. Ben was in shock. He did not anticipate this altercation. He wondered, how did she find out. More importantly, how was he going to get her to forgive him?

Since his classes were over, Ben drove back to Fairville. He now understood Wanda's point of view. He also knew that he loved her and did not want to lose her. When he arrived in Fairville, he went to the event center to talk to his mother.

Ben said, "Mom, I messed up with Wanda today."

Mom smiled and said, "You all had an argument."

Ben said, "It was big, she is very angry with me. No, she said that she was hurt. You know that's the last thing I wanted to do."

Mom said, "I know. What did you do?"

Ben said, "Last week she mentioned that her federal grant money was not enough to cover her housing and meals. I donated money to the university and asked Dean Smith to create a scholarship that Wanda would qualify for."

Mom said, "Oh, so she is upset with you for going behind her back."

Ben said, "Yes, she said that I did not believe in or trust her enough to figure it out on her own. That I tried to deceive her. That if I deceived her once, I would probably do it again."

Mom said, "I can understand where she is coming from. Why didn't you just offer her the money?"

Ben said, "I knew that she would not take it."

Mom said, "So, you were just going to force it on her."

Ben lowered his head and said, "I guess I was."

Mom said, "Making sure she had the money was going to make you happy."

Ben said solemnly, "I guess so. I didn't want her to struggle or go without."

Mom said, "I know. Just because you want to help someone does not mean that you need to help them. We all grow and mature when we have to figure things out. As much as I did not want to make you and your siblings work around the house. I had to. For one, I could not do it all myself. Two, you all had to learn how to do things. All training begins at home. I had to train you for when you would be on your own. Wanda has been trained well and knows how to maneuver in this world."

Ben said, "You're right. Grandpa told me once, that you can't over give to people. It spoils them and does not help them develop."

Mom said, "That's right. The goal is to teach a person to fish, not just give them fish when they are hungry."

Ben asked, "Do you think Wanda will forgive me?"

Mom said, "Of course she will. She loves you."

Ben said, "Mom, I love her too. I believe she is the one for me."

Mom said, "Of course, only you know what is in your heart. Wanda is a wonderful, young lady."

Ben said, "I know this seems quick. We have only been dating for a little over a month, but it's right. What do you think I need to do concerning Wanda being mad?"

Mom laughed and said, "Give her the time she needs and pray!"

They both laughed.

The next day Ben had meetings regarding the new sporting goods store. He decided that he would combine the two shops and call it 'Cason's Sporting Goods.' Demolition was done on the new building. It was starting to look great. Frank McCants was doing a great job. He hired an interior decorator to lay out the store. He was very pleased with the plan. Ben placed the order for all of the display cases, the merchandise, and everything else he needed.

Ben had not heard from Wanda, usually they would talk on the phone at night. On Wednesday, he was busy at the store. He explained to everyone that the store would be closed from November to February to incorporate the old store into the new one. The grand opening would be held on March

3, 1979. Just when Ben was about to close the store, Wanda walked in.

Ben smiled and said, "I really missed you Wanda."

Wanda said, "I missed you too."

Ben said, "I'm really sorry for hurting you, please forgive me!"

Wanda said, "I've had some time to cool down. I talked to Dean Smith, he convinced me to take the scholarship. He said that it was not set up just for me. The scholarship had stipulations, just like all of the other scholarships, and I qualified."

Ben smiled.

Wanda said, "I also realized that what you did was out of love and not malice."

Ben stepped a little closer.

Wanda said, "I need your promise that you will never do anything like that again."

Ben smiled and asked, "Let's say hypothetically that one day we are married and I can afford it. Are you saying you don't want me to surprise you with a tutoring center?"

Wanda smiled and said, "No! Reason number one, I'm not interested in opening a tutoring center anymore! Reason number two, if I were interested, part of the joy would be laying out the center like I would want."

Ben laughed and said, "OK, I won't do that!"

Wanda laughed and stepped closer to Ben.

Ben hugged and kissed her.

Ben said, "I know we haven't been dating long, but I have fallen in love with you."

Wanda said, "I feel the same way."

Ben laughed and said, "I'm glad. You know, you're very feisty when you get angry!"

Wanda smiled and said, "Yeah, I guess I am!"

Ben said, "I like it!"

Wanda asked, "Do you get angry much?"

Ben said, "No, I don't. I guess I take after my mom. I address every situation that I'm not happy with. If I can't resolve it, I pray that God will fix it or deliver me from it."

Wanda said, "That's a good plan."

Ben asked, "Will you be staying at your Uncle Robert's house tonight?"

Wanda said, "Yes, I plan to drive back to Macon tomorrow. My first class is not until 9:30 am."

Ben smiled.

Wanda asked, "Would you like to come over for dinner tonight? Dee is cooking!"

Ben said, "It doesn't matter who is cooking, I just like spending time with you. Let me call my mom and let her know I won't be home for dinner."

Wanda smiled and asked, "On Labor Day weekend, you think you can go to Warner Robins with me. I want to introduce you to my parents."

Ben asked, "Can we drive down after work on Saturday? I can close early. We can stay Saturday night and Sunday night."

Wanda said, "That would be fine."

Ben said, "Wanda, I have to ask you. How did you figure out that it was me that initiated the scholarship?"

Wanda said, "Dean Smith saw me in the hallway and asked me to come by his office after class. I did. He offered me the scholarship, I was excited. When I left his office, I went to the restroom. When I was leaving the building, I heard him telling his secretary that his 'favorite business student' had donated money for this scholarship. Everybody knows that you're his favorite business student."

Ben said, "Thanks, I could not figure it out. I knew that Dean Smith would not have told you."

Wanda laughed and said, "God tells me what I need to know. So, you better be careful."

Ben laughed and said, "I've learned my lesson!"

When they arrived at Wanda's Uncle Robert's house, dinner was ready.

Mr. Knowlton said, "Ben, I'm so glad you could come for dinner. My daughter's cooking is getting better."

Ben said, "Dee, dinner was delicious. Chili dogs was one of the meals I cooked before I started working at the golf shop."

Mr. Knowlton said, "I didn't know that you cooked."

Ben said, "I can put a meal on the table, some better than others. I don't have the gift like David does. When I started working and he started cooking, he embraced it."

Dee smiled and said, "He gave me some tips about cooking, before he left for the Institute."

Wanda said, "My grandmother taught me to cook. I, too, have not embraced it. However, like you, I can put a meal on the table, some better than others."

Everyone laughed.

Mr. Knowlton said, "When my wife died, I had to figure it out. A lot of nights I served Dee boxed macaroni and cheese and hot dogs."

Dee laughed and said, "I still like that meal!"

Wanda asked, "Uncle Robert, have you thought about dating again? Auntie Sara passed away about ten years ago."

Dee interjected, "Miss Saunders at the middle school likes my dad."

Ben said, "I remember her, the school secretary. She's a very nice lady."

Mr. Knowlton said, "Yes, she is a very nice lady. I do like her, but I can't ask her out."

Wanda asked, "Why not?"

Mr. Knowlton said, "I just don't think you should date people who work at the same company that you do. When things don't work out, there can be a lot of drama."

Ben asked, "Mr. Knowlton, are you eligible for retirement?"

Mr. Knowlton said, "At the end of the year I will be, but I need to keep working. Dee will be going off to college soon."

Dee said, "I understand your hesitation, but I think you should still ask her out. You never know, it might work."

Everyone laughed.

Ben stood up and said, "The least I can do is wash the dishes."

Wanda smiled and said, "We can wash them together."

Dee leaned back and said, "I won't argue with that!"

Mr. Knowlton said, "Me neither! Dee hasn't learned to clean as she goes. So, the kitchen is a mess."

Everyone laughed.

Mr. Knowlton was right. The kitchen was a mess.

After cleaning the kitchen, Ben asked, "What time do you plan to leave in the morning?"

Wanda replied, "Around 7:30 am."

Ben said, "I will stop by around seven o'clock to see you off."

Wanda said, "You don't have to do that!"

Ben smiled, kissed her forehead, and said, "I want to."

Dinner was delicious and fun. Ben said goodnight to everyone and left feeling very happy. When he got home, he told his mom that Wanda had forgiven him.

Mom said, "I knew she would. Did she accept the scholarship?"

Ben said, "Yes, she realized that it was not given to her. The scholarship was just available and she qualified for it."

Mom said, "I'm glad. She's a wise, young lady."

Ben smiled and asked, "What is Mary working so diligently on at the table?"

Mom said "You remember last year the movie 'Roots.' A lot of the teachers have created assignments for students to trace their family tree. So, she's looking at funeral programs of deceased family members to trace the genealogy as far as she can."

Ben said, "That's a great assignment. I can't wait to hear what she finds out."

3

MEETING THE PARENTS

The next couple of weeks flew by. Mom was busy at the event center. Mary finished her project.

While having dinner on Friday night before Labor Day, Mom said, "I can't believe how busy I've been at the event center. People are coming from all over to schedule events. I have bookings all the way into February of next year."

Ben said, "That's great. Mr. Stevens said that you would be busy."

Mom said, "It's only been a month and the news about the event center has spread like wild fire."

Everyone laughed.

Mary said, "I finished my family tree assignment. You won't believe what I found out."

Mom asked, "Do you want us to guess?"

Mary said, "Even if you had one thousand guesses, you would never guess this."

Ben said, "Don't keep us hanging."

Mary said, "I was able to trace our family tree on Mom's side all the way back to 1865."

Mom said, "That's wonderful."

Mary said, "In the lineage are regular people, all trying to provide for their family nothing out of the ordinary. However, when I got to 1865 that's when I could not go back any further. However, I found a birth certificate."

Ben asked, "OK! Mary, are you drawing this out for dramatic effect?"

Mom laughed.

Mary said, "One of our ancestors is Jeremiah Thomas Baldwin."

Mom said, "That name sounds familiar."

Mary said, "You remember, Grandpa told us that when his parents moved down from New York City, that they met a man in Atlanta. His name was John T. Baldwin. That man gave his parents shelter until Grandpa was born in 1892. He also helped him find a home and start a business. Then Grandpa's father helped him start a business."

Mom said, "Yes, I remember. He also said that John T. Baldwin was lynched in 1905 for having that blacksmith business."

Mary asked, "Yes, but do you remember that John T. Baldwin had a brother?"

Ben asked, "Are you saying that Jeremiah Baldwin was John T. Baldwin's brother."

Mary exclaimed, "That's exactly what I'm saying."

Mom said, "Mary, if that's true, then our family helped Grandpa's parents when he was born. Then we helped Grandpa at the end of his life."

Ben said, "Mary, that's mind boggling."

Mom said, "No, that's God. Our families have been intertwined from the beginning."

Mary said, "I know. We were not the first black family to love Grandpa, our ancestors loved him too."

Ben asked, "Was it hard to find this information?"

Mary said, "The funeral programs were a great start. It listed all the family members of the deceased. So, I was able to go back three generations. Then when I had a name and needed a parent's name, I was able to go down to the courthouse and look it up on the microfiche. Once I had a name, I could find the birth certificate. It was easy because our family stayed here in Fairville."

Mom said, "Mary, you have done great work."

Mary said, "Thanks! I don't think I will include the connection to Grandpa in my report. Nobody but us cares about that."

Mom said, "That's wise. However, it's confirmation for us that God continues to order our steps."

Ben said, "I agree. Remember, tomorrow I'll be going to Warner Robins to meet Wanda's parents."

Mom said, "I'm sure they will love you."

Ben said, "I'm a little nervous."

Mom said, "Black men are very protective of their daughters. Wanda is an only child, so I'm sure her father is very protective."

Ben said, "I can only be me."

Mom said, "That's more than enough. Remember, her father wants to make sure that you are treating his daughter with respect, that you are able to provide for her, and that you will support her goals as well as your own."

Ben said, "Thanks for the heads up."

Mary said, "I have decided what type of man I will marry."

Mom laughed and said, "Oh you have! What type of man do you want to marry?"

Mary said, "I want him to treat me like my brothers do and Grandpa did. I want him to be able to cook, I don't plan to cook all the time. I want him to be ambitious. He doesn't have to have a lot of money, but I want him to have some ideas on how to get more. Of course, he has to be intelligent to keep up with me."

Mom and Ben laughed.

Mom said, "That's a good list. Sometimes we don't fall in love with people that meet our specifications."

Mary said, "Well, I don't plan to settle on those things. It doesn't matter to me if he's tall or short, black or white, American or French. However, he has to do those things."

Mom asked, "Have you put your desires in your prayer?"

Mary said, "Yes, I have!"

Mom said, "God says a man finds a good wife. So, I'm sure, he will find you."

Mary said, "Good, I don't have time to look for him!"

Everyone laughed.

The next day Ben worked hard in the golf shop to close early for his trip to Warner Robins. Everything was going according to plan. His bags were packed and he was on schedule to pick up Wanda in front of her dorm at five o'clock. He decided to get gas before he left Fairville. When he got in his truck, it would not start. He tried several times to crank it. This was the third time his truck would not crank. On the previous two occasions, he had a mechanic from the auto repair shop fix it. It was something different each time. He looked under the hood and did not see anything out of the ordinary. His truck was almost nine years old.

It was now three o'clock and the auto repair shop had closed. He did not want to miss this trip to meet Wanda's parents. He walked over to the Chevrolet dealership.

The salesman asked, "Can I help you with anything?"

Ben said, "I would like to buy a truck."

The salesman said, "We don't have many used trucks!"

Ben said, "I don't want to buy a used truck. I want to purchase a new truck."

The salesman asked, "Aren't you Ben Davis from the golf shop?"

Ben said, "Yes I am. I would like to purchase a truck."

The salesman asked, "Will you need financing?"

Ben said, "No!"

Confused the salesman said, "Let me get my manager."

Ben waited impatiently. He did not want to be late picking Wanda up.

The manager said, "Hi, my name is Tommy Savor. I understand you want to purchase a truck."

Ben said, "I do, but I don't have a lot of time. I own a 1970 Ford F-150. It has been giving me problems. I want to trade it in on a new truck."

Tommy Savor asked, "Well, have you decided what truck you want?"

Pointing to his left Ben said, "Yes, I would like that blue 1979 Silverado, fully loaded."

Tommy Savor said, "That's a nice truck. I sold Mr. Cason the last car and van he bought about a year ago."

Ben relaxed and smiled.

Tommy Savor said, "He picked out the vehicles he wanted and brought me a certified check on the next day. Would you like to do the same?"

Ben said, "Great! However, I won't be able to bring you a certified check until Tuesday when the bank opens. I can write you a check now for a down payment."

Tommy Savor said, "I trust you, that will be fine. Let's get you in that new truck."

Tommy told the salesman to prepare the truck for delivery and to fill it up with gas. Ben gave Tommy a check for the down payment. He signed a document denoting he would be back on Tuesday to finish the paperwork.

Ben said, "Mr. Savor, I can't tell you how much I appreciate your help. When I need some other vehicles, I will be sure to come back."

Tommy Savor said, "Great! I look forward to doing business with you. When do you plan to open the sporting goods store? I have to drive to Macon to get equipment for the soccer team I coach."

Ben said, "Our grand opening will be Saturday, March third of next year."

Tommy Savor said, "I look forward to it. You may not remember me, I graduated from high school a year before you did."

Ben asked, "Now that you mentioned it, do you have a younger brother named Timmy?"

Tommy said, "Yes, I do. He was in your class. He's in the army now."

Ben said, "I remember. I'm sorry. I was so frustrated earlier. I have a date and my truck would not crank. Thank you so much for your help. I will see you on Tuesday."

Tommy said, "I look forward to it."

Ben said, "I'll get the truck running on Tuesday and bring it over."

Tommy said, "Don't worry about getting it fixed. I'm sure it's something small, since it was running before. We can have a tow truck come pick it up on Tuesday."

Ben said, "Tommy, you have been a great help to me today. Thank you!"

Ben got in his new 1979 blue Silverado.

Tommy waved and said, "Have a great time on your date!"

Ben drove back to the shop and got his suitcase. He could still make it to Macon and not be too late picking up Wanda. As he pulled in front of the dorm, it was 5:20 pm. Wanda was waiting out front.

He got out of the truck and said, "I'm so sorry that I'm late."

Wanda said, "No problem, I knew something must have happened. You bought a new truck!"

Opening the passenger door Ben said, "Yes, I had not planned to, but my truck has been giving me problems. Today it would not crank. I knew my mom needed her car this weekend. So, I didn't have a choice."

Wanda said, "It's very nice. Did you know that blue was my favorite color?"

Ben laughed and said, "No! I didn't, but I'm glad that it is!"

Wanda said, "So you just walked over to the Chevrolet dealership and bought a new truck. How much money did your Grandpa leave you?"

Ben smiled and said, "Enough to buy this truck!"

The trip to Warner Robins was quick. It was only thirty-five miles away.

Wanda said, "Don't be nervous, I'm sure my parents will like you."

Ben asked, "Could you see that I was nervous or are you just encouraging me?"

Wanda said, "I could tell. When you're nervous, you fidget."

Ben laughed and said, "I do. No one else has ever noticed. If they did, they never told me."

Wanda said, "You're the first boy, I have ever introduced to my parents."

Ben smiled and said, "I want to be the last!"

As they drove up to house, Mr. Knowlton was working in the yard. Ben opened the door for Wanda and retrieved the luggage from the back.

Wanda ran to greet her father, giving him a hug, she said, "Hi Dad!"

Mr. Knowlton said, "How's my baby girl doing?"

Smiling Wanda said, "Dad, this is Ben Davis."

Mr. Knowlton extended his hand and said, "Hi Ben, it's great to meet you. Come on in the house."

The house was very nice. It was bigger than his home. Ben stood at the front door holding the luggage.

Mr. Knowlton yelled, "Denise! Wanda and Ben are here!"

Mrs. Knowlton rushed out of the kitchen to hug her daughter.

Wanda said, "Momma, this is Ben Davis."

Mrs. Knowlton hugged Ben and said, "I have heard so much about you. I'm happy to meet you."

Ben tried to relax and smile. He placed the luggage on the floor.

Mr. Knowlton asked, "Did you eat already. Denise has prepared dinner."

Ben replied, "No sir, we have not eaten."

Mrs. Knowlton said, "Good, dinner will be ready very soon. I have the bread in the oven."

Ben asked, "May I use your restroom to wash up."

Mr. Knowlton said, "Wanda, show him where the restroom is."

When Ben came out of the restroom, he felt better. He

took a deep breath and walked into the dining room where everyone was seated.

Mrs. Knowlton said, "Ben, please sit right here."

Ben smiled and took his seat. Mr. Knowlton said grace and started passing around the food.

Ben said, "This looks delicious."

Mrs. Knowlton said, "Thank you, let's see how it tastes."

Ben smiled.

Mr. Knowlton said, "Ben, my brother, Robert, has told us a lot about you. What can you tell me that he has not already told us?"

Ben said, "Wow, Mr. Knowlton has known me for as long as I can remember. He goes to my church, so he knows my family. He is also one of my mentors, so, he knows all about me. I guess he doesn't know that I bought a new truck today."

Everyone laughed.

Ben said, "I had not planned to buy one. My old truck had been giving me problems, today it would not crank. I didn't want to miss meeting you this weekend. So, I bought a new one."

Mrs. Knowlton said, "You can't plan for everything."

Mr. Knowlton said, "I saw the truck when you drove up. It's very nice. Did you get a good deal?"

Ben said, "Yes sir, I did."

Wanda asked, "Can Ben relax now that you know everything about him?"

Mr. Knowlton said, "Please relax Ben. Robert told us all about you. He told us about your mom, Mary, and David. He even told us that Dee has a crush on your brother."

Everyone laughed.

Mrs. Knowlton said, "He has also witnessed how you treat Wanda. He's very pleased, so we are pleased too."

Ben said, "Thank you. I care a lot about your daughter."

Mr. Knowlton said, "It's obvious."

Mrs. Knowlton said, "I can see that she cares a lot about you too."

Mr. Knowlton asked, "Do you fish?"

Ben said, "I have only been fishing one time. Before my father died, he took me fishing when I was ten years old."

Mr. Knowlton asked, "Would you like to go fishing tomorrow morning before church? Or is that too early for you?"

Ben smiled and said, "No sir, that sounds like fun."

Everyone enjoyed the weekend. Ben and Mr. Knowlton caught a mess of fish. They caught mullet, brim, and catfish. Wanda and her mother prepared the fish for dinner after church. On Monday before Ben and Wanda left, plans were already made for them to come back to visit in November. They would also spend a few days in December after Christmas. As they drove away, it was bittersweet. Ben could see that Wanda was happy.

He said, "I had a great time with your parents. They're very nice."

Wanda said, "They had a great time too. My mother told me not to let you get away."

Ben laughed and said, "I don't plan on going anywhere."

Wanda smiled.

4

THE LETTER

After the trip to Warner Robins, Ben was working hard trying to get everything done. He burnished the display case. He had not done that in a while. Mr. Jennings and Mr. Stevens presented to him a plan to build the movie theater, Putt-Putt golf, and bowling alley. They also suggested that some additional commercial suites be built to lease out. This would generate more revenue. Ben loved the plans. Mr. Jennings found an architect and contractor to build the complex. The plan was to start building October 1, 1978 and to finish the project no later than April 1, 1979. Ben was extremely pleased.

Between customers Ben tried to do some homework. The graduate classes were very challenging. Then Ben remembered that he never read the last letter from Grandpa. He had placed the letter in the keepsake cache he kept in the storage room. He retrieved the letter and started to read it out loud.

Ben,

If you are reading this letter, then you know that what I turned over to you was more than just the golf shop. I'm sure you were surprised to learn all that I had. I trust you Ben. I know that you will take what I had to the next level. It all belongs to you now. I'm glad God gave me someone to save it for.

There is one thing that Hank did not tell you about. Really no one knows but me. The display case that I keep in the shop. You know it has a lot of sentimental value because my dad gave it to me. What you don't know is how valuable it really is.

I told you and the family the story about John T. Baldwin. He was a good friend to my father. They would go hunting and fishing in the woods of Fairville. After hunting one day, they returned to the land that my father owned and they decided to dig a pit to roast the wild boar they had killed. They dug the pit. In the spot where they dug, they found a confederate army bag. Of course, this was 1895, so the war was over. They determined that it had been buried there during the Civil War. In the bag were some gold bars. John T. took the gold and melted it down. He created the display case that you know about. My father had a dream to open a golf shop. There were some other things that he also created. In my house you will find two large candlestick holders. They are made of pure gold too. John T. made some candlestick holders and other things for himself. When John T. was killed, my dad was very sad. When times were hard, my dad sold some of the small things to get money.

*About twenty years ago I found a man in Atlanta,
he was willing to buy the gold if I ever needed it. His
name is George White. I checked in January 1978.
He still had his shop; he was training his grandson to
take over for him. I told him about you. He said that
if you ever needed money for the gold, he could get
it for you. His business card is enclosed in this letter.*

*I have no doubt that you will continue to build
the portfolio. I just wanted you to know about your
safety net.*

*As you know I kept the display case in the shop.
I know that you will be expanding the store, so it may
no longer be safe there. Whatever you do, I trust you.*

*You know that I love you and I am very proud
of you. I could not love you any more if you were my
own flesh and blood. Because of you my last six years
were the happiest years of my life since my wife passed.
Continue to follow your intuition. I know that God
has a woman for you. I pray that you find her soon.*

I Love you,
Grandpa!

Tears rolled down Ben cheeks. He could not believe that
God had given him something else. His cup was running over
with all of the businesses, yet God continued to bless him.

He picked up the display case and said, "You can no longer
stay here in the shop. I can't take the chance that someone will
steal you. Grandpa almost had a heart attack that time a few
years ago when Mr. Green's son broke into the shop."

Ben closed the shop and drove to the bank. As he walked
into the bank, everyone was looking at him carrying the display
case.

The bank teller asked, "May I help you?"

Ben said, "Yes, I need a safe deposit box which is large enough to hold this."

The bank teller said, "We do have a very large drawer. Please have a seat and I will get someone to help you."

Ben waited patiently. He completed the forms and was taken to a room where the safe deposit box was located. The monthly cost to rent the box would automatically be deducted from his personal account.

Ben said under his breath, "Good that I can't tell anyone about everything. This story is becoming more unbelievable each day."

Ben left the bank feeling better about the safety of the display case. He planned to pick up the candlestick holders and put them in the safe deposit box tomorrow.

Weeks flew by and the seasons started to change. He hired Mary to help him out in the shop on Saturdays. She enjoyed it. Her only problem was talking to the customers too much.

This was Mary's junior year, she was taking French. She was doing well. She was also preparing to take her SAT test. Mom was very busy at the event center. She found a caterer in Harrisburg who was willing to cater events, but he was not as good as David. People complained.

Ben and Wanda continued to go on dates every Friday and Saturday night. They visited her parents again in early October. Things were going great. Her parents enjoyed spending time with him. He also enjoyed spending time with them. He realized that he loved fishing. It was not only relaxing, but very rewarding. He was never sad if they did not catch anything, he just enjoyed the process.

5

I DON'T WANT TO BREAK UP!

David came home for a long weekend in October. He looked different: taller, thinner, and stronger. He continued to excel at the Institute. He was learning so much.

Mom asked, "Are you eating enough? You look thinner."

David said, "I haven't lost any weight, but I have grown about two inches. I also started running."

Mom said, "Running. I thought you didn't like running. When I asked you if you wanted to run track, you said no."

Everyone laughed.

David said, "I didn't want to run then. However, you need great endurance to work in the kitchen for eight hours. One of the guys started a running club. I joined and it has helped me handle those long days in the kitchen."

Mary said, "You do look thinner, but I like it."

Mom said, "I like the clean shaven look on you. Why did you shave your mustache?"

David laughed and said, "If you have facial hair in the kitchen, you have to take additional steps for sanitary purposes. I decided to shave it off while I was in school."

Everyone laughed.

Ben said, "Wanda and I are taking Mary and Becky to the state fair on Saturday. Would you like to come?"

David said, "I would like that. Is Dee going?"

Mary snickered.

Ben said, "I'm sure if we asked, she would love to go."

David said, "OK, count me in. Mom, you want to go?"

Mom said, "No thank you! I don't like crowds anymore. I will be happy to stay right here. Anyway, I have an event Saturday night. Everyone keeps asking me when will you be available to cater. They're having a hard time finding a good caterer to come to Fairville."

David said, "Wow, that's great. I'll be home on December second. I don't have to go back until January thirteenth. So, I could do some catering then."

Mom said, "That would be great."

Ben said, "I have to go back to work for a little while, I'll see you all later tonight."

Ben had locked up the shop, but was working on some order forms, when there was a knock at the door. He looked up, it was Wanda. He rushed to open the door and gave her a hug.

Confused Ben asked, "Wanda, I thought I wouldn't see you until tomorrow, when I picked you up for the fair."

Wanda said, "I know that was the plan, but I needed to see you. There's been something on my mind that we should talk about."

Ben said, "No problem! I was just completing some order forms. Let me finish this last one and we can talk about whatever you want."

Ben quickly did some calculations and completed the forms. While he worked, he saw Wanda pacing the floor.

He stopped working on the form, went to her, and asked, "Wanda, what's wrong? What has you so worried?"

Wanda asked, "Did you finish your calculations."

Ben said, "No, I noticed how worried you looked. What's wrong?"

Wanda said, "You know how much I care about you."

Ben said, "Yes! You know how I feel about you."

Wanda said, "Yes. We've been dating now for four months. I love how close we're getting."

Ben said, "I do too."

Wanda asked, "How do you feel about premarital sex?"

Ben said, "Truthfully, I don't believe in it. I made a vow to wait until I got married. I know some people may think it's old fashioned."

Wanda exclaimed, "Thank you Jesus! I feel so much better. I made a vow to wait too. I was worried, that you would want to break up with me because of my belief."

Ben hugged Wanda and said, "I can't believe that you were worried about that."

Wanda said, "I was. I didn't want to continue our relationship and then one day I said no and you wanted to break up."

Ben said, "I also felt we needed to talk about it. I was just waiting for a good time to bring it up."

Wanda said, "My roommate broke up with her boyfriend on Monday, because he was pressuring her to have sex. It made me think about you."

Ben said lovingly, "I'm sorry to hear that. You should know that even if I had not made a vow; I would never pressure you."

Wanda said, "I felt that, but I needed to make sure. If we were going to break up, I wanted it to be soon. I didn't want to continue to fall deeper in love with you."

Ben smiled and said, "I made a vow during the summer of 1972. I was in Vacation Bible School."

Wanda interrupted, "I was here that summer; that's when I made my vow. Sis. George was teaching the Ten Commandments. She spent a lot of time on fornication and adultery. A lot of the kids were laughing. I didn't want to intentionally sin, so I made a vow to wait until I got married."

Ben smiled and said, "I did the same thing."

Wanda said, "I have been in prayer all week concerning this. I was so worried."

Ben pulled Wanda closer and said, "Wanda, I can't imagine my life without you. My prayer has been that God will give us many years together."

Wanda smiled and said, "I love you Ben."

Ben smiled and said, "I love you more."

He pulled Wanda close and took his time trying to kiss her as lovingly as he could. He wanted her to feel the love he had for her. When he finished, Wanda stepped back.

Wanda said slowly, "Ben, that kiss! I've always loved the way you kiss me, but that kiss was full of. Full of! It was so full of love. I could feel it."

Ben said, "I'm glad. I don't want you to ever be concerned about how much I love you."

Still trying to recover from the kiss, Wanda said, "Please, don't kiss me like that all the time."

Ben smiled and said, "No, I plan to kiss you like that each day we are together."

Wanda laughed.

While stepping over to the counter, Ben looked back at her and asked, "Have you found it difficult to keep your vow?"

Wanda said, "No, I haven't. I think God has been keeping boys away from me. I had one boyfriend in high school. He broke up with me when I said no. While I was in junior college, I lived at home. So, I did not socialize as much. I worked and went to class. When I got to Middle Georgia State, a lot of guys noticed me, but I was not impressed by any of them. Then, when I came to Fairville, there was you."

Ben laughed and said, "I'm glad God kept the boys away from you."

Wanda asked, "Have you found it difficult?"

Ben said, "No, not really. During high school, I didn't have a girlfriend. Once I started working at the golf shop, all I did was work, go to church, and go to school. When I was at college, I didn't meet anyone that I was interested in being close friends with except Tammy. It was the summer before my second year that I finally asked her out."

Wanda asked, "So you and her did not …"

Ben said, "No, we both agreed to wait until we were married."

Wanda said, "At first when you didn't make a pass at me, I thought that you did not find me attractive. After a while, you made it clear that you did."

Letting out a deep breath Wanda said, "I feel so much better now!"

Ben said, "Wanda, I have always found you attractive. Don't think that I haven't thought about it. When I do, I pray and push those thoughts out of my head."

Wanda laughed and said, "You always make me feel beautiful when I'm with you."

Ben said, "That's easy! You are. You're not just beautiful on the outside, you're beautiful on the inside too. Sometimes I look at you and the beauty within you is shining through. You're very thoughtful, generous, loving, unselfish, and compassionate. I could go on."

Wanda smiled and said, "Thanks Ben. Each time I think I can't love you any more, you do something to make me fall in love with you all over again."

Ben smiled and said, "Good!"

Wanda said, "I know some girls; they broke up with their boyfriends because the guys made them feel unappreciated, unwanted, unvalued, unloved, and unsupported. You have never made me feel that way. When I'm with you, I feel appreciated and wanted. You encourage me and then support me in my decision. I also feel that you value my contributions to whatever we are doing."

Ben said, "I'm glad you feel it. I do appreciate and value you. I do try to encourage and support you. I also want you by my side."

Wanda smiled.

Ben said, "When I'm with you, you make me feel like I can do anything. Of course, I know that I can't. However, you motivate and encourage me. You challenge me to be a better man; I like that. Yet, I don't feel pressure from you if I haven't figured it out yet. You believe in me and are willing to help me."

Wanda said, "I do believe in you, I believe in us. I think we are good for each other. We complement each other."

Ben said, "Yes, we do. Do you have any more questions?"

Wanda laughed and said, "No, I'm good!"

Ben said, "David is home and he wants to go to the fair with us tomorrow. Do you think Dee wants to go?"

Wanda laughed and said, "I'm sure she will, if David is going."

Ben drove Mom's car to the fair because it was bigger. Ben, Wanda, and Mary sat in the front. David, Dee, and Becky sat in the back. Everyone had a great time at the fair. Mary and her best friend, Becky, went their way. David and Dee went their way. Ben and Wanda were on their own. Wanda won a stuffed animal throwing the baseball. Ben was impressed.

Ben said, "You're pretty athletic. Did you play sports while in high school?"

Wanda said, "Yes, I played basketball and ran track."

Ben asked, "Do you still run now?"

Wanda said, "I don't, but I have been thinking about starting up again. I ran the other day when I was stressed."

Ben laughed.

Wanda asked, "Would you like to run together?"

Ben said, "Yes, I would. Now, I don't want to run a marathon."

Wanda laughed and said, "No problem, I don't like running long distances. Three miles will be fine with me."

They ate funnel cakes, fried Oreos, chicken on a stick, and drank at least a gallon of lemonade. When it was time to leave, everyone was exhausted. Wanda took pictures.

Mary said, "I had a great time."

Wanda asked, "Who was the boy, I saw you talking to?"

Mary said, "Oh, his name is Jason. He goes to my school. He has a crush on me."

Everyone laughed.

David asked, "Do you have a crush on him?"

Mary said, "No. He does not meet my standards."

Everyone laughed.

6

HOLIDAY SEASON 1978

The weeks flew by fast. Ben closed down the golf shop on November 1, 1978. It would be closed until the grand opening on March 3, 1979. Due to the upcoming closing, during the month of October, he kept the shop open seven days a week. People came from all over. It seemed like every customer, who received a coupon that was mailed to them, brought it in for their discount. He was able to deplete most of his inventory. The items that were left, he put them on the 'marked down' table.

Even though the store was closed for renovations, Ben was still busy during the month of November. If he was not setting up the new store, he was reviewing plans for the bowling alley, Putt-Putt golf, and movie theater. For Thanksgiving, David was home for an entire week. He catered two parties at the event center. Mom had him booked for fifteen events during the month of December.

Mom had about twenty servers on call. Dee, Pam, Mary, Joyce, Debra, and Becky were making good money serving events. Mom started cooking Thanksgiving Dinner on the

Monday before. She invited Wanda, her uncle Mr. Knowlton, his daughter Dee, and Miss Charlene Saunders, the secretary for the middle school, to dinner. Our house was too small for that many people, so she served dinner in the small room at the event center.

David said, "Mom, this is a big perk for managing the event center, we get to use it ourselves."

Everyone laughed.

Mr. Knowlton said, "Phyllis, thanks for the dinner invite. I didn't want to cook dinner this year."

Charlene Saunders said, "I appreciate the invite too. My sister lives in Macon. She had invited me to dinner. When I go there, she is always trying to fix me up with someone new."

Everyone laughed.

Mom asked Mr. Knowlton to say grace. After grace, everyone ate until they could not eat any more. The food was delicious.

David said, "Mom, I forgot how good your cooking is. I have been cooking so much when I came home."

Miss Saunders said, "Phyllis, everything was delicious. Thanks for letting me make dessert. I wanted to contribute something."

Mom said, "I didn't want to worry about dessert. So, when you volunteered, it was easy to say yes."

Mom put the cakes and pies on the table. Everyone enjoyed the desserts.

Mr. Knowlton said, "Charlene, you're a great baker. This cake is delicious. David, this is better than your cakes."

David said, "I know. Miss Charlene, you're going to have to tell me your secret."

Everyone laughed.

Wanda and Ben could not keep their eyes off each other.

Mary noticed and said, "Why do you two keep looking at each other? What's going on?"

Ben smiled and said, "Mary, you need to stop looking at everybody."

Mary said, "You didn't answer my question!"

Wanda said, "I'm not looking at Ben any more than usual."

Dee said, "I agree with Mary, something is up!"

Ben said, "If you must know, Wanda and I are celebrating our five-month dating anniversary, that's all."

Mom said, "That's nice."

Mary leaned over to Dee and said, "Something else is going on!"

David said, "I have some good news. I found a company who wants to bottle my spaghetti sauce. They'll let me use my name."

Mom said, "David, that's great news."

Ben said, "Remember, don't sign anything until Mr. Jennings reviews it."

David said, "I won't. It's nice to know that someone is interested."

Mary said, "I'm not surprised. What do you want to call your spaghetti sauce?"

David said, "I have a few names, but nothing great yet."

Mary suggested, "How about 'David's Awesome Spaghetti Sauce'?"

David said, "That's not bad, I'll add it to the list."

Mr. Knowlton said, "David, this is a big accomplishment. I'm very happy for you."

David said, "Thanks!"

Mom said, "If you say yes to this company, how long would it take before bottles are on the shelf?"

David said, "It could be as early as next fall."

Ben said, "Congratulations, David. I'm very proud of you."

David said, "Thanks! It's been hard work."

Mom said, "However, you did it. What's next on your list?"

David said, "I have written my business plan to start a catering service. I have also written the business plan to open a cafe'. All I have to do now is graduate. That will be two and a half more years."

Charlene Saunders said, "Don't rush it. You're at the Institute for a reason, don't rush it."

Mr. Knowlton said, "Charlene is right. The curriculum is four years for a reason, you're only half done with all they have to teach you."

David said, "I know."

Wanda said, "I have some good news. I have been offered a scholarship to go to graduate school in the fall."

Dee said, "That's great news. I didn't think you wanted to get your master's degree."

Wanda said, "I'm still not sure. I see how hard Ben is working. However, it's nice to be offered the scholarship."

Mom said, "Congratulations Wanda. Do you have a date for your graduation yet?"

Wanda said, "Yes, I do. It will be the fifth of May."

Mom said, "We will be there."

Wanda said, "I want to plan a dinner the night before graduation."

With her mouth full Mary said, "We will be there too!"

Everyone laughed.

Mr. Knowlton asked, "Ben, when will you open the new store?"

Ben said, "March third, it can't come fast enough."

Mr. Knowlton said, "I know that opening a new store is

not easy. I worked in a retail store when I first graduated from college. We opened a new store. It was a lot of work."

Dee said, "Dad, I didn't know that. I thought you were always a teacher."

Mr. Knowlton said, "I didn't start teaching until after I married your mom. She was from Fairville. So, if we wanted to live here, there were not many jobs available."

Charlene Saunders said, "I know what you mean. I had the same dilemma when I moved here."

Mr. Knowlton said, "The good thing about you opening the sporting goods store is that you will be able to provide more jobs in the community."

Ben said, "Yes. I'm very excited about that."

Mom said, "I just heard that the church received a substantial donation."

Mary asked, "Do you know who it's from?"

Mom said, "No, I don't. Robert, do you know who it's from?"

Mr. Knowlton said, "No, I don't. I'm just glad we did. We received the benevolent donation about a month ago. The pastor has approved the Deacon's recommendation to combine the donation with the existing building fund and build a larger fellowship hall with and an educational wing. We have already found a contractor. We hope to start building in January. It should take about three months to complete."

Ben smiled and said, "That sounds great."

After dinner, everyone helped clean the area and kitchen. Ben and Wanda were working together.

Ben asked, "Do you think if I offered your uncle a job at the sporting goods store, he would take it?"

Wanda asked, "What job?"

Ben said, "I need an assistant manager. I can't keep doing everything myself."

Filled with dismay Wanda said sadly, "I thought you would hire me."

Ben hugged her and said, "I have other plans for you. In order for those plans to work, I'll need someone else to run the store day to day."

Wanda laughed and said, "Apparently, you don't want to tell me those plans yet. As long as I will be working with you, I'm OK with that!"

Ben pulled Wanda closer and said, "You're right, I can't tell you now. Trust me you will be right by my side."

Wanda smiled.

Ben said, "I love working with you. I think we can do great things here in Fairville."

Wanda smiled and said, "I do too! I think you should ask Uncle Robert. He said that he was eligible for retirement and if he's not working at the school, maybe he will ask Miss Charlene out. I like her."

Ben said, "I was thinking the same thing."

Mom had takeout containers and aluminum foil available for everyone to take food home. When the team was finished, the place looked shiny and new again.

On the next day, Wanda and Ben planned to go Christmas shopping in Macon. Ben arrived at her uncle's house a little earlier, Mr. Knowlton opened the door.

Ben said, "Hi, I know I'm a little early to pick up Wanda. I was hoping to talk to you about something."

Mr. Knowlton said, "No problem come on in. Please have a seat. Is anything wrong?"

Ben said, "No sir, all is fine. As you know I plan to open the new store on March third."

Mr. Knowlton said, "Yes, I'm very happy for you."

Ben said, "I need an assistant manager. Would you be interested in the job? I can offer you ten percent more than whatever you're making now."

Mr. Knowlton said, "Ben, I haven't worked in the retail industry for over twenty years."

Ben said, "I know, but I need someone I can trust. We can learn the industry together. You said that you were eligible for retirement soon."

Mr. Knowlton said, "Ben, this is a good offer. Let me pray on it and I'll let you know."

Ben said, "I know this is a new store, but I truly believe it will be successful. So, there is very little risk."

Mr. Knowlton said, "I agree. I believe the store will be successful too. You could possibly start a chain."

Ben said, "I was thinking the same thing. However, I can't do anything unless I have someone that I can trust running the store. If things go like I pray it will, in about a year you could be manager. That would free me up to work on the other stores."

Mr. Knowlton said, "Give me the weekend, I'll let you know my answer on Monday."

Ben said, "That would be fine. Thanks for coming to dinner yesterday. I had a great time."

Mr. Knowlton said, "I did too. I'm glad Phyllis invited Charlene. I know she was trying to set us up."

Ben smiled and asked, "Did it work?"

Mr. Knowlton said, "I have to admit, I do enjoy her company."

Ben laughed and said, "If you worked at the store, you would be free to date her!"

Mr. Knowlton said, "I know!"

Wanda entered the room and said, "Ben, I didn't know you were here. Have you been waiting long?"

Ben stood up and said, "No, I was just talking to your uncle. You look beautiful as always."

Wanda said, "Thanks! Are you ready to go?"

Ben said, "Yes. Mr. Knowlton, we'll see you later."

Mr. Knowlton said, "Have fun!"

When they got in the truck, Ben said, "I offered your uncle the assistant manager position."

Wanda asked, "Did he take it?"

Ben said, "He's going to pray about it."

Wanda said, "I think he will. He and Miss Charlene had a great time yesterday."

Ben said, "I noticed that too. Where do you want to go shopping?"

Wanda said, "I want to go to Montgomery Ward and Sears."

Ben said, "No problem. Have you figured out gifts for everyone yet?"

Wanda said, "Not everyone, but I do have a list."

Ben and Wanda shopped until they dropped. At the end of the day, they had purchased gifts for her family and his family.

Mr. Knowlton accepted the job and agreed to start on February 1, 1979. Ben was excited. The next few weeks went by fast. David was home and ready to cater. Wanda was on Christmas Break from college, she spent most of the time in Fairville. Ben took her to all of his meetings concerning the new store. She helped him make some important decisions about color, layout, and placement of displays.

They decided to spend Christmas Eve with his family, but Christmas Day with her family. They planned to stay in Warner Robins for four nights. They would return to Fairville for New Year's Eve to attend watch night service at the church. On Christmas Eve, David cooked a light meal. It was delicious.

Mom said, "Since Ben won't be here tomorrow. I was thinking we should exchange gifts tonight."

Mary said, "I like that."

Mom said, "I don't want to make this a habit, but I wanted us to exchange gifts together."

Wanda said, "I'm glad."

Mom said, "I don't want to open gifts too early. How about eight o'clock?"

David said, "That's fine with me."

Everyone helped clean the kitchen. After the kitchen was cleaned Ben and Wanda went for a walk.

Ben said, "My legs are sore from running."

Wanda laughed and said, "Mine are too. I don't think we were ready for five miles yet."

Ben exclaimed, "I tried to tell you! I'm glad that I'm not the only one sore."

Wanda said, "You're a good athlete. Why didn't you participate in sports during high school?"

Ben said, "Once I started working at the golf shop, I enjoyed spending time with Grandpa. I also did not want to give up the money I was making. I was able to help my mom with the bills and save money for college."

Wanda asked, "Have you always been this responsible?"

Ben said, "I think so. As the oldest, I had to watch David and Mary. Yes, I had a lot of responsibility, but I never resented it or felt it was an imposition. I enjoyed helping, I love my family."

Wanda drew closer and said, "You're amazing. I'm glad that God brought us together."

Ben smiled and said, "Me too!"

When Ben and Wanda finished their walk, it was almost eight o'clock. Mary was on the porch, waiting for them to come home.

Mary exclaimed, "Come on, it's almost time!"

When everyone was gathered in the living room, Ben said, "Mom, Wanda and I are going to exchange gifts with each other tomorrow. I hope you don't mind."

Mom said, "I don't mind. Wanda, I want you to call me and let me know what he got you."

Everyone laughed.

As she passed out her gifts Mary said, "I will go first. Usually I get the same thing for everybody. This year, I didn't."

Everyone laughed.

David opened his gift first, it was a very nice tie. It was decorated with cooking utensils.

David said, "Mary, this is a very nice tie. I like it. Last week, we had to dress up for a dinner. Next time, I'll wear this tie."

Ben opened his gift. It was a tie too! His tie was decorated with different sports.

Ben said, "Mary, I don't know where you got these ties. Even though they are funny, they are very nice. I really like it. Thanks!"

Mary laughed and said, "I did not get Wanda and Mom a tie!"

Everyone laughed.

Wanda opened her gift to find a framed picture of her and Mary.

Wanda said, "Mary, I love this picture. We took it at the fair."

Mary said, "I like it too. You're like a big sister to me. I love you."

Wanda said, "I love you too. You know I'm an only child.

That's why Dee and I are so close. Now, God has given me you! Thank you!"

Mom finally got her gift opened. She found an eleven-inch by fourteen-inch depiction of their family tree. Mary had filled in all of the names of family members all the way back to 1865. She also put Grandpa's name next to Mom's real father's name."

Mom wiped the tears from her face.

Mom said, "Mary, this gift is so thoughtful. I love it. It's a memorial to all of our family that came before us. You even included Dad's name. Thank you, Mary."

Mary hugged her mother. Mom passed around the framed family tree for everyone to see.

David stood up and passed out his gifts.

David said, "There are so many places to shop in Atlanta. It can be overwhelming."

Wanda said, "I heard people at the university talking about how they go there to just shop. Several have talked about what good deals they found."

David exclaimed, "It's amazing."

Mary opened her gift first. It was another bookbag.

Mary exclaimed, "David, thank you so much. I have worn out the bookbag Grandpa gave me. I needed another one."

David said, "I found this shop that was full of them. I figured that you needed another one. I had worn mine out too."

Everyone laughed.

Wanda said, "I saw Ben's purple one and wondered where got it. That's very nice. Are they popular in Atlanta?"

David said, "Yes, they are. I saw a group of kids get off the bus. Half of those kids had a book bag."

Mary said proudly, "When Grandpa gave us our first book bag three years ago, he said that they would be very popular."

Mom finally got her gift open. She found a very pretty ring and bracelet.

Mom said, "David, this ring is beautiful. I have never seen anything like it."

David said, "It's a mood ring. The stone will turn colors depending on your mood. The bracelet will do the same thing."

Leaning over Mary said, "I want to see!"

Ben said, "I read about those rings. If it's blue, that means you're happy."

Mom said, "Well, mine should be blue all of the time. You know blue is my favorite color."

Everyone laughed.

Mom said, "Thank you David. I love it."

Wanda opened her gift from David. It was a mood ring and bracelet too.

Wanda said, "David, I'm so glad you got me one. Just then I was thinking, I want one too. Blue is my favorite color."

Everyone laughed.

Wanda said, "The ring is adjustable, I really do like it. Thanks!"

Ben finally opened his gift, it was five different Rhythm and Blues (R&B) albums on cassette.

Ben said, "I really needed this. My new truck has a cassette player in it and I did not have any tapes to listen too. Oh, you got Earth, Wind, and Fire, The O'Jays, Rick James, LTD, and James Brown. Thank you, David. I love it."

David said, "I bought the same ones for me. I listen to them in my room in the evening. I've really enjoyed them."

Mom stood up and said, "I will go next."

She distributed her gifts.

Mom said, "Well, I did a Mary this year. All of you got the same thing."

Everyone laughed.

Mary rushed to open hers first. It was a track suit.

Mary said, "This is the new fashion now. Everyone has a track suit that they wear when they don't want to dress up. I love it. I love it. Thanks Mom!"

David opened his gift to find a red track suit.

David said, "I really needed this too. Since I've been running, it's been very cool in Atlanta. I can also wear it when I just want to run to the store or something. I love it. Thanks Mom."

Wanda opened her gift to find a blue track suit.

Wanda said, "I love it too. Did you know that blue was my favorite color?"

Everyone laughed.

Ben opened his gift to find a navy blue one.

Ben said, "Mom, I do like it. Wanda and I are running now too. On those days when it's cold, we can wear it. Thanks, Mom."

Mom said, "I'm glad you like it. David, I got you an extra-long length since you're getting so tall."

David smiled and said, "I'm sure it will be fine."

Looking at Ben, Wanda stood up and said, "I guess it's our turn."

She passed out the gifts that she and Ben had bought for the family. Mary opened hers first. It was a pair of Calvin Klein jeans.

Mary exclaimed, "I can't believe you got me a pair of designer jeans. Everyone at school has them. I really wanted a pair. Thanks Ben and Wanda! I love it!"

Mom said, "Those are very nice. I'm sure they will look great on you."

David opened his gift to find a gray Members Only jacket.

David said, "Wow! These jackets are lightweight, but look so nice with jeans. Thank you, Ben and Wanda. I love it."

David tried on the jacket and said excitedly, "The sleeves are long enough. Thank you!"

Mom finally got her gift open. It was a beautiful gold watch.

Mom said, "This watch is beautiful. It's a Seiko. You should not have."

Ben said, "We wanted to get you something very nice. We saw this watch and thought it would look beautiful on your wrist."

David and Mary oohed and awed.

Mary said, "Mom, you mentioned the other day that your old watch was not keeping good time."

Mom said, "I did say that. Thank you, Ben and Wanda, it's beautiful and I love it. I'm only going to wear it on special occasions."

Ben said firmly, "No, we want you to wear it every day!"

Mom stood up and said, "OK, I will. Thank you all for the beautiful gifts. God has blessed me with a wonderful family and I'm grateful."

Everyone stood up and hugged Mom.

Looking at the Christmas tree, Mary said, "There's another gift under the tree."

David said, "Oh, I got Dee something."

Everyone snickered.

Mary asked, "What did you get her?"

Mom lightly hit Mary on the shoulders and said, "Mary, that's none of your business."

David said, "It's OK. I just got her a cook book. She told me that I wanted to cook something different."

Ben said, "That was nice of you David."

Wanda said, "She's going to love it."

Everyone laughed.

On Christmas Day, Ben and Wanda drove the two-hour drive to Warner Robins. It was early afternoon when they arrived. It was a cold, rainy day. Ben could not remember the last time it rained on Christmas. When they got in the house, Ben placed the presents under the tree. Everyone greeted him with a hug.

Ben said, "I'm glad we got here before it started raining hard."

Mrs. Knowlton said, "I am too. The forecast said that it would be raining for the next two days."

Mr. Knowlton said, "I had planned for us to go fishing tomorrow."

Ben said, "We will be here until Friday morning. So hopefully, the weather will clear up."

Wanda asked, "Momma, do you need any help in the kitchen?"

Mrs. Knowlton said, "No, I have been waiting to open gifts. I'm glad that you all are here."

Ben said, "Great, I'm excited. Before we open gifts, Mr. Knowlton, I want to show you something in the truck."

Sitting down in his favorite chair, Mr. Knowlton said, "OK, let me put some shoes on."

Mrs. Knowlton asked Wanda, "What does he have in the truck?"

Wanda said, "I don't know. I thought we brought in all of the gifts."

Ben and Mr. Knowlton stepped outside.

Ben opened the passenger door of the truck and said, "I really don't have anything out here to show you. I want to marry your daughter. I plan to ask her when we exchange gifts.

I just wanted to get your blessing. I should have said something the last time we were here."

Mr. Knowlton smiled and said, "No problem. I have no reservations. You have my blessing. I could not be happier for you."

Ben said, "Thank you sir!"

Mr. Knowlton said, "Now, you're going to wait till after she finishes her degree to have the wedding?"

Ben said, "Yes. I just did not want to wait any longer to ask her. I know we have only been dating for six months, but I know that she's the one for me."

Mr. Knowlton said, "I asked Denise to marry me after four months. She said it was too soon. So, after two more months I asked her again. Then she said yes."

Ben laughed.

Mr. Knowlton said, "Now, Denise is going to ask me what you wanted to show me in the truck."

Ben said, "You can tell her about the cassette tapes I have."

Mr. Knowlton laughed and said, "That's weak, but that's all we got."

Ben laughed.

When they returned to the living room. Mrs. Knowlton asked, "What was in the truck?"

Mr. Knowlton looked at Ben and said, "Nothing major, he just wanted to show me his new cassette tapes."

Trying to divert the conversation Ben asked, "Is everyone ready?"

Wanda said, "Yes."

She passed her mother and father their gifts. Mr. Knowlton rushed to open his gift. It was a very large box. He found new fishing gear inside. There were lures, hooks of different sizes, fishing line, and a retractable fishing pole. All of the gear was in a really nice black pouch.

Mr. Knowlton said, "I like this. I love the retractable fishing pole. I can't wait to try it out. Look! There are lures, hooks, a knife, and everything else I need right in this one bag. I love it. Thank you, Ben and Wanda."

Mrs. Knowlton was having trouble opening her gift, Wanda helped. When it was finally opened, she gasped.

Leaning over to see Mr. Knowlton asked, "Denise, what did you get?"

Mrs. Knowlton said, "It's a beautiful gold watch. I love it."

Wanda said, "When we saw the watch, we knew that both you and Ben's mom would love it. So, we bought two, one for each of you."

Mrs. Knowlton said, "Well, I hope she liked hers as much as I like mine. The strap on my watch broke last weekend. I needed another one. I would have never splurged and bought me one so fancy."

Mr. Knowlton asked, "Is it a Timex?"

Mrs. Knowlton said proudly, "No, it's a Seiko!"

Mr. Knowlton oohed.

Everyone laughed.

Mr. Knowlton stood up and said, "We have some gifts for you."

He gave Ben and Wanda their gifts.

Wanda said, "Dad, I hope you did not buy me jewelry again!"

Mrs. Knowlton said, "No, he didn't. I told him that you had enough earrings and necklaces."

Everyone laughed.

Wanda finally got her gift open and found a jewelry box. Wanda held up the box and said, "Dad, it's beautiful."

Mr. Knowlton said, "Well, you needed something to hold all of the jewelry."

Everyone laughed.

Mrs. Knowlton said, "I told you to get her a very nice frame for her degree."

Mr. Knowlton laughed and said, "I know, but I liked the jewelry box better."

Wanda said, "I love it. I did need somewhere to keep all of my jewelry. I was using a plastic tray to hold it."

Ben opened his gift to find a very nice Chevrolet Silverado stainless steel keychain. It was a cutout of the truck.

Holding up the keychain Ben said, "I love it. It looks just like my truck. I needed a new keychain. I would have never bought this for myself. Thank you so much!"

Mrs. Knowlton said, "I thought that you would like it since you just got your truck."

Ben smiled and said, "I do. I love it."

Ben and Wanda hugged her parents.

Mr. Knowlton asked, "Have you all exchanged gifts yet?"

Wanda said, "No, we wanted to exchange them here with you."

Mrs. Knowlton smiled and said, "Well, go ahead. I can't wait to see what you got each other."

Wanda said, "I will go first."

She passed Ben a beautifully wrapped gift.

Ben asked, "Wanda, did you wrap this?"

Wanda smiled and said, "Yes, I did."

He said, "This is the prettiest gift, I have ever received. I don't want to open it."

Mr. Knowlton said, "I want you to! Open it!"

Everyone laughed.

Ben tried not to mess up the wrapping paper. He understood

now why his mother opened her gifts so carefully. Finally, he got it open without tearing the paper or destroying the bows. When he opened the box, he found a memory book. It documented all of the things they had done over the last six months.

Ben said, "Wanda, I love it. You captured everything we have done together. There are pictures. You even have our first date, when you beat me in bowling."

Wanda said, "Yes, I have been working on it for a while."

Ben said, "These memories are cemented in my mind, but I love the way you laid them out. You're a good scrapbooker. I love it."

Wanda said, "There're a few empty pages, we can fill in as we go."

Ben said, "I love that idea. Thank you!"

He stood up and hugged Wanda as lovingly as he could with her parents right there.

Mrs. Knowlton said, "Wanda, that was a beautiful idea."

Mr. Knowlton said, "I agree. Wanda, it's a beautiful gift."

Ben said, "Well, I guess I'm next."

Wanda sat back down on the sofa. Ben took Wanda's hand and gently pulled her, so she could stand next to him.

He said, "Wanda, you know how much I love you."

Wanda said, "I know."

Ben said, "These last six months, I have been happier than I ever thought I could be. Remember, I prayed that God would give us many years together."

Wanda said, "I have been praying that prayer too."

Ben pulled the ring out of his pocket and dropped to one knee. Wanda covered her mouth with her right hand.

Ben asked, "Wanda, will you marry me?"

Mr. Knowlton reached over and took his wife's hand.

Wanda said, "Ben, of course I will marry you. I love you."

Ben placed the ring on Wanda's finger.

Ben said, "If you don't like it, we can exchange it."

Wanda said, "I love it, it's beautiful."

Ben kissed Wanda.

Mr. Knowlton and Mrs. Knowlton smiled, cheered, and clapped their hands.

Wanda asked, "Ben, how did you know my ring size?"

Ben laughed and said, "I read that a woman's shoe size is most likely her ring size. So, I took a chance."

Mrs. Knowlton exclaimed, "Wanda, let me see the ring!"

Wanda walked over to her mother.

Mrs. Knowlton said, "Ooh! This is a beautiful ring. It's a two-carat pear shaped solitaire, approximately D or E on the colorless scale, and internally flawless. It's very, very nice!"

Looking at Mrs. Knowlton, everyone laughed.

Walking back over to Ben, Wanda kissed him and said, "I love you, Ben."

Ben said, "I love you more."

Mr. Knowlton asked, "Now, isn't it good that I bought that jewelry box?"

Everyone laughed.

Ben and Wanda had a great time in Warner Robins. They decided to get married in July 1979 in Fairville at the Cason's Celebration Center. They would check the event calendar for the exact date. Mr. Knowlton and Ben got a chance to go fishing. Everyone had a great time.

7

THE GRAND OPENING

B en and Wanda decided to get married on July seventh at one o'clock in the afternoon at the Cason's Celebration Center. It took a lot of work for Ben to convince Wanda to let him pay for the wedding. He told her that he came in underbudget for the store expansion; she finally let him deposit money into her account.

Robert Knowlton, Wanda's uncle, started working at the store in February. He was a great source of information for Ben. They worked well together. He suggested to Ben that he call him Robert. Out of respect, Ben continued to call him Mr. Knowlton.

Everything was on schedule. The new building was completed. All of the merchandise was ordered, they were just waiting for stock to come in. They interviewed for cashier, custodial, and stocker positions. Mary, Dee, and Pam were sad that they could not work at the store. Mom kept them busy at the Celebration Center.

A total of fifteen positions had to be filled, eight full-time and seven part-time. Ben hired employees that were both black and white, male and female, young and older. Wanda trained the cashiers on customer service, upselling, the new cash register, and the processing of credit cards. She created a process for the cashiers to cash in and cash out. All team members were issued three uniform polo shirts with the store logo on it. The shirts were blue and white. Team members had to wear black pants, no shorts.

There would always be at least two cashiers on cash registers. Other cashiers would walk through the store to help customers. Wanda created work schedules that would cover ten o'clock in the morning until six o'clock in the evening, Monday through Saturday. Ben decided to close the store on Sunday.

Security cameras were installed. Ben requested that the police department provide deputies on sight the first week. Wanda coordinated a balloon and face painting station in the front of the store for kids. There would also be free hotdogs and punch for customers from eleven o'clock in the morning until one o'clock in the afternoon. Ben mailed out another letter to loyal customers reminding them of the grand opening with a coupon attached. Robert advertised in the paper every Sunday for the month of February and submitted a writeup to the Macon radio stations. Wanda hired a photographer to take pictures at the grand opening.

Finally, March third had arrived. All team members had to be at work at eight o'clock that morning. Ben gathered the team in the break room for prayer. Ben thanked God for everything. He prayed that workers would not be overwhelmed and customers would come back again. Mr. Knowlton rallied everyone together with a chant. All of the team were excited about this opportunity. Wanda walked to the front to unlock the door at ten o'clock in the morning and there was a crowd waiting outside.

She screamed, "Everyone get ready, we have a crowd already."

As she opened the door, she smiled and greeted everyone. Ben came to her side and hugged her.

Wanda said, "You did it!"

Ben pulled her closer and said, "We did it."

The morning went by fast. The store contained sporting goods for baseball, soccer, football, basketball, and track. There was a special area for golf equipment, it was called Cason's Corner. There was sport clothing, socks, and tennis shoes available. There was professional paraphernalia for the Atlanta professional ball teams.

There was also a separate table where a customer could be added to the mailing list to receive future coupons. There was a lot of noise in the store, but it was a good noise. Ben and Wanda thanked the customers as they left the store. The photographer took a great picture of the couple standing in front of the store.

Wanda made sure all team members took their breaks on time. She filled in at the cash registers when needed. She also walked the store to encourage customers to try different products.

There was a steady stream of customers all day. At six o'clock, Ben locked the door. All of the team members were assigned an area to clean and reset. At six thirty, Ben invited everyone into the break room. The deli department of Piggly Wiggly donated dinner for all employees. Everyone sat around the table to eat and discuss the activities of the day. Wanda recorded suggestions to improve various areas. Finally, at 7:15 pm, all of the team members left the store. Ben, Wanda, and Robert all hugged each other.

Robert said, "Ben, everything went so smoothly today. I was so surprised."

Ben said, "I know. I could not believe it. Even the small hiccups that we had were fixed very quickly. There was a sense of peace in the store, no discord."

Wanda said, "My adrenaline is still high. Today was great. I'm so proud of our team members. I know it was a long day, but they worked hard."

Ben said, "I could not stop thanking God. As I walked through the store, I was just so thankful."

Robert said, "God was in this place today. I got a chance to talk to a lot of the white customers. They were so impressed by the store, the merchandise, and the customer service. Many of them said they were very happy the store was in Fairville."

Ben said, "I noticed that sixty-five percent of the customers today were men. One woman told me that we did not have anything for her."

Everyone laughed.

Wanda said, "I will research some products for women that are not sport related that we can carry."

Robert said, "That's a great idea. Aerobics is a big thing now, maybe we can carry some of those products."

Ben said, "That's a wonderful idea. I also think we need a 'marked down' area. We can push some of the products that are not moving or obsolete."

Wanda said, "I was thinking we could stock some impulse buying items. Those items that grab the customer's attention when they are checking out."

Ben said, "I ordered some chips and candy but they won't be delivered until Monday."

Robert said, "Well, we have tomorrow off. One lady asked me if we were going to be open tomorrow. I explained to her that we would be closed on Sundays. She asked why. I explained that would be our day of rest. She said, you're missing out on more sales. I told her that we are willing to take the chance."

Ben said, "I don't think we will be missing out on sales. If God can bless Chic-fil-a, he can bless Cason's Sporting Goods too!"

Everyone said, "Amen!"

When they were walking to the car, Ben said, "Wanda, I noticed that you didn't eat today. Are you OK?"

Wanda said, "You're right. I didn't eat. I was too excited, but I'm hungry now."

Ben said, "When David was in the store, he said that he would save dinner for us."

Wanda said, "Great. I can't believe you noticed that I didn't eat."

Ben laughed and said, "I have 'Wanda-vision'. When you're nearby, I notice everything about you."

Wanda kissed him and said, "I guess I have 'Ben-vision'!"

Ben said, "Good!"

On Monday, the store was just as busy as it was on Saturday. On Tuesday stock had to be reordered.

Ben said, "I thought we had enough inventory for a week."

Robert said, "I know. I don't want to order too much; our stock room is not big."

Ben said, "The next store we open needs to have a larger storage room."

Robert said, "I will start a list of things to include in next store."

Ben said, "That would be great. Mr. Knowlton, I'm so happy you took the job. I needed you."

Robert said, "I'm glad I did too. Charlene and I are a couple now. I really like her. I regret not saying something to her earlier."

Ben said, "God's timing is perfect. I'm glad that you two are doing well."

Robert said, "This is going to be a busy year. We have the store, Wanda's graduation, and the wedding. That's just takes us to the summer."

Ben smiled and said, "I know. I've decided not to take graduate classes during the summer. I don't want to worry about it while we are on the honeymoon."

Robert asked "Have you decided where you want to go?"

Ben said, "I'm working on it. I have a few ideas."

Robert asked, "Where do you plan to live?"

Ben said, "I have Grandpa's house. I didn't do anything with it. He said his neighbors were prejudice, so I'm not sure."

Robert said, "You could live there temporarily, while you build a house."

Ben said, "That's a good idea. I don't want to talk to Wanda about that now. I will wait until after the wedding. She's busy getting ready for the graduation and wedding."

Robert said, "She is very excited. You should hear her and Dee talking about the wedding plans."

Ben said, "I'm excited too. Remember, tomorrow is Wednesday. I have classes. Will you be OK by yourself?"

Robert said, "Yes, I will be fine. I like the team members we hired. They're all hard workers. I do think we need to schedule the part-time employees more hours this week."

Ben said, "That would be great. I expect the first two weeks to be hectic, but I think that it will settle down then."

After his classes on Wednesday, Ben met Wanda for lunch.

Wanda said, "I really enjoyed working at the store. My mind has been racing all week trying to come up with innovative ideas to improve."

Ben said, "I know. Maybe we should have waited on the

wedding since we had the grand opening. Your graduation is also coming up."

Wanda said, "No, I don't want to delay marrying you. I can handle it. I have been running. It has helped me not be stressed."

Ben said, "July seventh is not that far away."

Wanda said, "Oh, I realized this morning, that July seventh is the day that your grandfather died. Do you want to pick another day? We have time to change the invitations if you do."

Ben said, "No, I don't want to pick another day. I knew that it was the same day. I'm not sad when I think about Grandpa. I'm happy. I'm fine with that date."

Wanda smiled and said, "I like the date too."

Ben said, "Please, let me do more for the wedding?"

Wanda said, "Really the wedding is not an issue. We already chose the invitations. They will be mailed out on the first of May. My roommate helped me find a dress. I picked out the bride maids dresses. David is catering for us. Since we are having the wedding and the reception in the same place that makes it easier. I don't need a lot of flowers, we will be using the wedding arch. The florist will decorate it on the day before and bring the bouquets and boutonnieres when she comes. Rehearsal is already scheduled for the evening before. The disc jockey has confirmed that he can be there. So, there is not much left to do."

Ben said, "That's true. I just don't want you to be overwhelmed."

Wanda said, "I'm not. I really enjoy the coordinating. The photographer we hired for the grand opening, he will also do the wedding. Oh, did you confirm with Reverend King that he could marry us?"

Ben said, "Yes, I did. I heard that some people have their ceremony videotaped. What do you think?"

Wanda said, "I like that. Can you find a videographer?"

Ben smiled and said, "Yes, I can."

Wanda asked, "Have you decided where we are going on our honeymoon?"

Ben said, "Since you are leaving it up to me, I have a few ideas. So, I want it to be a surprise."

Wanda said, "I don't know what to pack."

Ben said, "Pack for summer weather. We are not going up north."

Wanda laughed and said, "Well, hopefully we won't be going outside much."

Ben exclaimed, "Wanda, I'm trying to wait! You're tempting enough, don't put thoughts in my head!"

Wanda laughed.

Ben asked, "What about dinner for your graduation?"

Wanda said, "I contacted Walton's Events like you suggested. She has a room that I can rent. I have a caterer. I made a list of who I want to invite, so everything is set."

Ben said, "I already rented a hotel room for that Friday night for my family, Robert, and Dee."

Wanda said, "Great. The money you put in my account was more than enough to take care of the wedding stuff and the graduation dinner."

Ben said, "Good!"

Wanda said, "I bought you a new outfit to wear for the graduation dinner."

Ben said, "Thanks!"

Wanda said, "I also found a tuxedo shop that has the tuxedo color we want. I just need you, David, Caleb, and Uncle Robert to go get measured. I have already paid for the rentals."

Ben said, "OK, great. I will get the guys over there."

Wanda said, "It's the tuxedo shop at the mall."

Ben said, "You have taken care of everything."

Wanda said, "I made a list and I'm checking the items off as I go."

Ben asked, "What about dresses for the mothers?"

Wanda said, "My mother found a dress in Warner Robins. Unfortunately, Fairville does not have many places to shop. So, your mother and I plan to go shopping on next Wednesday. She is going to ride to Macon with you. While you are in class, we will go shopping."

Ben said, "I say it again. You're amazing."

Wanda smiled.

Ben asked, "Did you want to have a bridal shower?"

Wanda said, "Not really, but your mother talked me into it. The women of the church are coordinating it. All I have to do is show up on June twenty-third. Are you having a bachelor party?"

Ben said, "No. The guys and I will hang out when we go to get sized for the tuxedos. That's fine with me."

Wanda said, "We have talked so much about the wedding. How is the store doing this week?"

Ben said, "It's going great. We had to place more orders to restock yesterday."

Wanda said, "I knew the store would be successful. I'm very proud of you."

Ben said, "Thanks, but I don't deserve all of the credit. You know that you played a vital role in this. I look forward to us working together all the time."

Wanda said, "Me too!"

Ben asked, "How are your classes going?"

Wanda exclaimed, "They're going great. These last classes are easy. I took the hard courses last semester."

Ben said, "You're just very smart!"

Wanda smiled.

Ben asked, "Have you thought any more about graduate school?"

Wanda said, "I have. I don't think I want to go. I may change my mind later. Right now, I don't."

Ben said, "That's fine. If you went now, we could have classes on the same day and drive up together."

Wanda said, "I didn't think about that. Let me pray on it some more."

Ben said, "Whatever you decide is fine."

Wanda said, "You know that I love you. It seems the more I love you, the more love I receive from you."

Ben laughed and said, "I feel the same way. I guess we can't out love each other."

Wanda laughed and said, "I guess not."

Ben said, "That's a good thing!"

Wanda said, "It's a great thing. I have to go now. I'll talk to you later tonight."

Ben hugged and kissed her, then said, "I love you."

Wanda smiled and said, "I love you more!"

Ben said, "That's my line!"

Wanda laughed.

8

MOVING FORWARD WHILE GIVING BACK

Time was going by fast. It was now the middle of April. The store was still very busy. A lot of the customers were from out of town. The Celebration Center was doing very well. The high school booked the large room for the prom. Mom was busier than she had expected. She had to hire a part-time assistant, just to get some days off. Mary took her SAT test. She felt good about it. Ben had a meeting scheduled with Mr. Jennings.

Mr. Jennings said, "Ben, I am so glad to see you today. Timothy has only great things to say about the sporting goods store and the Celebration Center."

Ben said, "The store is doing great. The Celebration Center has become very popular. It has only been open seven months, it's already turning a profit."

Mr. Jennings said, "I know. This is our first meeting since the bowling alley, Putt-Putt, and movie theater opened."

Ben said, "It was great. I am so pleased with everything. Of course, I knew everything that was going on. When Wanda and I went to the grand opening, I was still impressed. Thank you for everything."

Mr. Jennings said, "Those were some great ideas. Do you have any more?"

Ben said, "I do have some more. Hopefully, next year I will open another sporting goods store in Macon."

Mr. Jennings said, "That is wonderful. If you are interested, we can also sell franchises. You won't have to do the work to open, but other people will pay you to use your name and contacts."

Ben said, "Um, I will think about that. I would also like to open a storage place here in Fairville. If people want to store things, there is nowhere to do it. I think this would be another lucrative investment."

Mr. Jennings said, "I agree. We have land already. We can have that facility built in only a few months."

Ben said, "Well, I would like to pursue that next."

Mr. Jennings said, "I will get with Timothy and devise a plan."

Ben said, "As you know, Wanda and I will be getting married in July. I was thinking about where we will live."

Mr. Jennings said, "Well, you still have your grandfather's house. I can get some people over there to spruce it up. Paint the outside and inside, give it a fresh look."

Ben said, "That is a great idea. Grandpa said that some of his neighbors were prejudice."

Mr. Jennings said, "Yeah, one particular person, Mr. Morris Tucker, perished in January. So, he is no longer there. There still is Mrs. Agnes Boatwright. She is a sixty-five-year-old widow and she can be adversarial, surly, and not easy to deal with. At least she is not hostile."

Ben said, "I was thinking, Wanda and I could live there a little while until we built something else."

Mr. Jennings said, "I think that is a great plan. I will get some contractors over to the house. Have you cleared out everything valuable in the house?"

Ben said, "Yes, I have. That's why I wanted to build a storage unit. I had to take the furniture to Macon to store it. Right now, the house is somewhat empty. I did want to purchase a bedroom set and maybe a dinette set before the wedding."

Mr. Jennings said, "Let me work on it. I will get it looking very nice for you."

Ben gave Mr. Jennings the key to the house and said, "Thank you."

Mr. Jennings said, "Have you had your meeting with Timothy yet?"

Ben said, "No, I will see him next week."

Mr. Jennings said, "Well, I saw the fiscal report. You have increased your grandfather's portfolio. You have proven to be a very good business man. I think your net worth is up to about forty-five million dollars now."

Ben said, "I'm shocked."

Mr. Jennings said, "The sporting goods store, bowling alley, movie theater, Putt-Putt golf, and the event center are all making money. Keep up the good work."

Ben said, "I will try. I would also like to open a simple self-service car wash. We don't have one of those here in Fairville. It would not require a lot of management, but I think it would be a money maker."

Mr. Jennings said, "I agree. I will draft plans for that too."

Ben said, "I do think Grandpa would be proud of what I've done."

Mr. Jennings said, "I know that he would be. I'm very proud of you too. When your grandfather first told me that he wanted to leave everything to you. I was concerned. I knew that he did not have anyone else. The first day I met you, I was impressed and my reservations went away. I know that he's very proud of you."

Ben said, "Thank you sir!"

Mr. Jennings said, "Make sure you send me an invitation to the wedding."

Ben laughed and said, "Don't worry, you're on the list. They will be mailed out on May first."

Ben left the office feeling good about the meeting. When he got to the sporting goods store, the police were there. Someone had been caught shoplifting. It was a young, black boy about fifteen years old. The policeman gave Ben and Robert the report.

Ben asked, "Mr. Knowlton, what do you think about offering the young man a job?"

Robert said, "That's a great idea."

The policeman asked, "So you don't want to press charges?"

Ben said, "No, I don't. I want to give him a chance. We will monitor him closely, I think he just needs someone to invest in him."

Robert suggested, "We need a part-time custodian. Mr. Jones could use some help at night doing the floors."

Ben said, "That's a great idea."

The policeman said, "OK, I will take the handcuffs off of him and bring him back here for you."

Ben said, "Thanks!"

After a few moments, the young man was brought to the office.

Pointing at the chair in front of his desk Ben said, "Please, have a seat."

Robert asked, "What is your name?"

The young man said, "Joshua Thomas!"

Ben said, "I know what happened. I am willing to let it go this time. Are you interested in working here?"

Joshua sat up straight and asked, "You would hire me, when I tried to steal from you?"

Ben said, "Only if you are willing to work and not steal from me again."

Joshua said, "I don't know."

Robert said loudly, "Well, if you don't know. We can call the policeman right back in here."

Joshua said, "Oh, OK. Yes, I would be interested."

Ben asked, "What grade are you in?"

Joshua said, "Tenth!"

Ben asked, "How are your grades?"

Joshua said, "They're OK, I get C's. I could do better, but why? It's adequate."

Ben said, "If we offer you the job here, I expect you to do better in school."

Joshua asked, "How much better?"

Ben said, "The best that you can do. If you need help, we have someone here that will be willing to tutor you."

Joshua asked, "You would do that for me?"

Robert said, "Yes, we would, but you have to do your part."

Joshua said, "OK, I'm interested."

Ben asked, "Have you ever worked before?"

Trying to sit up straight Joshua said, "No real job. I have chores at home that I do sometimes."

Robert asked, "What type of chores?"

Joshua said, "I'm supposed to keep my room clean, I clean it up every now and then. I know how to mow the lawn. When I get tired of my mom complaining, I go ahead and do that. I take out the trash and clean the kitchen sometimes."

Ben said, "If we hire you, I expect for you to not only do better in school, but do the chores that you are assigned at home."

Joshua exclaimed, "What! You're asking a lot!"

Robert took a step forward and said, "The policeman is still waiting outside. I can call him in."

Joshua said, "OK, OK! I will try."

Ben said, "We will give you a job for one week. If we are pleased with your work, we will offer you the job for one month. If we are still pleased, we will let you work for three months. If at the end of three months, we are pleased. You have yourself a job for as long as you like."

Robert said, "I will also check with your mother to ensure you are doing your chores at home. I will check with your teachers to see if you are doing better in school."

Joshua exclaimed, "You're asking me to change everything about me!"

Ben said, "No, we are here to help you improve every facet of your life."

Robert said, "The job pays minimum wage, which is $2.90 an hour. We need help in custodial. You will work with Mr. Jones to clean the floors at night."

Joshua asked, "How often will I get paid?"

Ben said, "If you last more than one week. You will get paid each Friday for the week before."

Joshua said, "I can do that!"

Robert said encouragingly, "I believe you can do it too!"

Ben said, "The store closes at six o'clock. For the first week, you can work five o'clock to eight o'clock in the evening

Monday through Saturday with Mr. Jones. After the first week, we can figure out a schedule for the next month."

Joshua stood up and said excitedly, "Thank you. I won't let you down."

Robert smiled and said, "Come with me, I have some forms for you to fill out."

When they left the office, Ben asked God to help him be a good example for Joshua. Ben picked up the phone to make some calls. He called Tammy's parents.

Mr. Kennedy answered the phone.

Ben said, "Hello, Mr. Kennedy, how are you?"

Mr. Kennedy said, "Ben! I'm doing good. I hurt my back last week, but I'm better now. I heard about your grand opening, it was on our news here in Columbus. I saw a clip of you and your girlfriend, Wanda. She's a pretty girl. We're very proud of you."

Ben said, "Thank you sir. Things are going well."

Mr. Kennedy said, "I'm glad!"

Ben continued, "Sir, Wanda and I will be getting married on July seventh. The invitations will go out in May."

Mr. Kennedy said, "We're very happy for you Ben. I'm glad God had someone else for you. We'll try and come to the wedding."

Ben said, "It will be great to see you again."

Mrs. Kennedy took the phone and said, "Ben, thanks for calling and letting us know. We still love you and only want the best for you."

Ben said, "Thank you. I love you too."

Mrs. Kennedy said, "Paul has been trying to get in touch with you. He said you left a message for him."

Ben said, "Yes ma'am, I have been trying to call him. I only have his home number. Can you give me his work number?"

Mrs. Kennedy said, "Yes, it's (404) 535-5567."

Ben said, "Thank you so much, I'll stay in touch."

Mrs. Kennedy said, "Please tell your family hello for us."

Ben said, "I will. Goodbye."

Ben hung up the phone and called Paul.

Paul said, "Hello, this is Paul Kennedy."

Ben laughed and said, "This is Ben Davis, I have been trying to get in touch with you."

Paul laughed and said, "I'm never at home. Here in Atlanta, there is always something to do. How are you?"

Ben said, "I'm fine."

Paul said, "I saw you and Wanda on the news. The store looks very nice."

Ben laughed and said, "God has blessed. Wanda and I will be getting married on July seventh."

Paul exclaimed, "Congratulations! I'm so happy for you."

Ben said, "Thanks! Do you still sell real estate part-time?"

Paul said, "Yes, I do. You want to buy something in Atlanta?"

Ben said, "I do. I would like to buy a condominium!"

Paul said, "I can do that. Let me call you back in about fifteen minutes and we can talk."

Ben exclaimed, "OK, Paul don't forget about me!"

Paul laughed and said, "I won't, I just want to get some listings in front of me when we talk. I will call you right back."

Paul and Ben talked for a while. Ben told him what he was looking for. Paul planned to set up a time when Ben could come to Atlanta to view the different properties.

The next couple of weeks flew by. Joshua proved to be a very good worker. Mr. Jones was very pleased with his attitude and work ethic. Robert checked with his teachers. They said that Joshua was doing much better in class. He has shown more interest in assignments and have earned better grades.

Joshua's mother was very thankful. She said that Joshua's room was clean. She no longer had to ask him to clean the kitchen or mow the lawn. She could not believe the difference. She wondered if this was her son.

Wanda planned a dinner the night before her graduation. Everyone was there. Her parents, friends, Ben's family, some professors, and Dean Smith. The food was delicious. She hired a photographer.

Ben asked, "Is everyone here that you invited?"

Stepping closer to him Wanda said, "Yes. You look very nice tonight."

Ben said, "Thank you, someone thought I would look nice in this outfit."

Wanda laughed and said, "She was right. She needs to buy two more of the same outfit in different colors!"

Ben laughed and said, "You look even more beautiful than you did yesterday."

Wanda said, "Thanks, I tried something new tonight."

Ben said, "I see a different shade of lipstick."

Wanda exclaimed, "You noticed!"

Ben said, "Of course I did. I have 'Wanda-vision'."

Wanda laughed.

Everyone mingled and enjoyed the food.

After dinner Wanda stood up and said, "I am so glad that all of you could come celebrate with me tonight. I always knew that I would graduate from college. I just needed to execute my plan. As many of you know I attended junior college in Warner Robins before coming here to Middle Georgia State University. I am proud to say that tomorrow I will be graduating with honors, Magna Cum Laude."

Everyone applauded.

Wanda continued, "I am prouder that I have met all of you

on the way. I am thankful for you. As you know Ben and I will be getting married in July, so my plan is to move to Fairville. I am still on the fence about graduate school, but I have not ruled it out."

Mr. Matthew Knowlton, Wanda's father, stood up and said, "Denise and I are very proud of the young woman that Wanda has become. She sets a goal, then she attains it. She has always been very independent and goal driven. Wanda, we are very proud of you."

Mr. Robert Knowlton, Wanda's uncle, stood up and said, "Wanda has been like a second daughter to me. I am also very proud of her. She has a lot of my mother's qualities and if you want to succeed, get Wanda on your team. Congratulations Wanda!"

Dean Smith, the head of the Business Department at Middle Georgia State University, stood up and said, "As Mr. Knowlton said, Wanda is very independent. She knows that she can do whatever she sets her mind to. That is a wonderful quality. I wish more of my students had. She is not only intelligent, but willing to work. Congratulations! Your future is very bright!"

Ben stood up and said, "I agree with all that everyone has said about Wanda. She is not only intelligent, a hard worker, innovative, ambitious, and beautiful. After spending just two weeks with her, I fell in love. I am just so glad that this wonderful woman fell in love with me too. Congratulations, sweetheart!"

Everyone clapped. Ben leaned over and kissed Wanda on the cheek.

Wanda stood up and said, "Thank you all for coming out tonight. Hopefully, we will see all of you again at the wedding. Before we leave, please join me in taking a group photo. Those of you who know me well, know that I love photos!"

Everyone laughed.

Everyone helped clean the room before they left.

Ben said, "Wanda, I don't like having to leave you at the end of the night anymore. I can't wait until we're married."

Wanda leaned into him and said, "Me neither!"

On the next day the graduation started on time. There were 1,233 students in Wanda's graduating class. Everyone was very proud of Wanda. Ben's friend, Caleb, was graduating too. He was also graduating Magna Cum Laude with his engineering degree. Caleb accepted a job in Atlanta with a prestigious engineering firm. He was very excited. He planned to start work in two weeks. He still had not found the right woman for him. He felt there was a woman waiting for him in Atlanta.

After the graduation, all of the family met at Wanda's dorm. Wanda had taken a lot of things home already. There was very little to pack in the car. She planned to go to Warner Robins for a few days. Everyone said good bye and got on the road to go home.

Ben said, "I checked out your car. Your oil is good and your tire pressure is fine. Wanda, call me when you get home."

Wanda said, "I will. Ben, you're spoiling me."

Ben said, "I spoil people that I love."

Wanda said, "I do too. So, I guess there's going to be a lot of spoiling going on!"

Ben laughed and said, "I guess there will be."

Ben kissed Wanda very passionately.

Wanda said, "Ben, your kisses are changing!"

Ben laughed and said, "I know. You got me thinking about our honeymoon!"

Wanda laughed and said, "Don't start putting thoughts in my head!"

Ben laughed and said, "I love you. Drive carefully!"

That night, Ben and Wanda talked on the phone.

Wanda said, "Ben, I have been thinking about life after we get married."

Ben asked, "Is there a problem?"

Wanda said, "No problem. We both want to have children."

Ben said, "Yes!"

Wanda said, "I want us to be a couple before we're a family."

Ben said, "I don't mind that!"

Wanda said, "I want to start taking birth control pills."

Ben said, "Oh, I had not thought about that. If we want to plan our family, I guess that's a good idea."

Wanda said, "Of course, if God blessed us to conceive, I would not be upset. I just want to make sure we're prepared."

Ben asked, "Have you talked to a doctor yet?"

Wanda said, "No, I have an appointment in a few days. I wanted to discuss it with you first."

Ben said, "Of course, I don't know much about birth control pills. I understand there are some risks."

Wanda said, "That's true. There are some risks, but complications are very rare."

Ben said, "I just don't want anything to happen to you."

Wanda said, "I feel good about this decision. There are a few different medications he can prescribe."

Ben asked, "OK, if at any time there are complications, do we have a consensus that you will stop taking the pill?"

Wanda said, "Yes, I agree."

Ben said, "OK! Oh! Mary got her SAT results."

Wanda asked, "How did she do?"

Ben exclaimed, "She scored higher than me, she got 1535!"

Wanda said, "Oh my goodness! Colleges are going to be pursuing her big time!"

Ben said, "She received a letter today!"

Wanda said, "World watch out! Mary Davis is on her way!"

Ben laughed.

9

THE WEDDING

The next few weeks flew by. The store continued to draw great crowds from local and out of town shoppers. Joshua Thomas was working full-time during the summer. Mary continued to receive letters from colleges trying to persuade her to attend their school, many offered full scholarships. She really wanted to attend the University of Georgia. She was waiting to see if they would offer her a scholarship.

David was home for the summer. He was busy catering events at the Celebration Center. He was making a lot of money. The company, that wanted to bottle his spaghetti sauce, was still interested. They mailed David a contract. Mr. Jennings had the contract to review.

Mom was very busy at the event center. She had to convert the part-time employee to full-time. The event center had been open for eleven months and was doing very well. There were at least six events a week. Some weeks had ten events scheduled. Sometimes there were two events going on at the same time.

The ladies in the church coordinated a beautiful wedding shower for Wanda. She was overwhelmed with love and gifts.

Ben decided that he and Wanda would go to Atlanta for their honeymoon. Atlanta was a two and a half-hour drive. Even if they were going to fly somewhere, they would still have to drive to Atlanta's airport. He did not want their first night to be filled with travel.

He realized that he needed a car. Wanda was starting to have problems with her car. He had just got it repaired at the end of May. He decided to stop by the Chevrolet dealership. As he walked in the door, he heard someone call his name.

Ben turned around and said, "Hello Tommy! I was just coming to see you!!"

Tommy Savor asked, "You aren't having problems with that truck, are you?"

Ben said, "No, I'm not. I love it!"

Tommy said, "Congratulations on the store, it's really nice. You have everything I need plus some."

Ben laughed and said, "Thanks. Remember, if you need anything that we don't carry, I can order it for you."

Tommy said, "That's good to know."

Ben said, "Remember, I told you that I would be back when I needed another vehicle. I want to purchase a car."

Tommy said, "No problem. Have you picked one out yet?"

Ben said, "No, I haven't. I was thinking about the new Malibu. This car will be for my wife."

Tommy said, "Yes, I met Wanda when I was at the store."

Ben said, "Yes, the wedding is on next Saturday. I know today is Friday. I meant to stop by the other day."

Tommy said, "No problem. I'm sure we can find something you like."

Ben said, "Her favorite color is blue."

Tommy said, "OK, if you turn around. There on the

showroom floor is a fully loaded blue 1979 Malibu. You think she will like it!"

Ben turned around, smiled, and said, "I like it! I think she will like it too. I hope the interior is not black!"

Tommy said, "No, it is not; it's a creamy tan. It also has leather seats."

Ben opened the door on the driver side and got in.

Tommy said, "It has adjustable leather seats, FM radio and a cassette player, AC, cruise control, anti-lock brakes, and power windows."

Ben said, "I really like this!"

Tommy said, "We also have a very nice, comparable Monte Carlo over there."

Ben said, "No, I think she will like this. The Monte Carlo sits too low."

Tommy said, "That is true."

Ben said, "I don't want to take it home today. I don't want anyone to see it."

Tommy asked, "What time is the wedding on next Saturday?"

Ben replied, "The wedding is at one o'clock."

Tommy said, "I'm working that day. What about I get the car detailed really good and bring the car to you? I can park it out front and give you the key."

Ben said, "That would be great. If you could come after two o'clock, the reception will be going on."

Tommy said, "I can also put a really nice sign on the back that says 'just married'."

Ben smiled and said, "I like that."

Tommy asked, "OK, would you like to test drive it today?"

Ben smiled and said, "Yes, I would."

Tommy said, "Let me go get the keys."

When Ben left the dealership, he was very happy. Everything was going according to plan. He had reviewed his list several times to make sure he had taken care of everything. Ben and Wanda decided not to have a rehearsal dinner. They would just walk through the process and let everyone go. As Ben walked back into the store, he smiled. The store had at least thirty customers.

Wanda said, "Hello baby!"

Ben kissed her lightly on the lips and asked, "Everything going OK?"

Wanda said, "Yes. All is well. I was thinking about after the reception, when we leave for the honeymoon."

Ben laughed and said, "You got honeymoon on the brain!"

Wanda smiled and said, "I must admit, I have thought about it a few times. Seriously, I was thinking when we get in the car. I don't want to wear my wedding dress in the car."

Ben said, "That's a good thought."

Wanda said, "So, I bought us outfits that we can travel in."

Ben said, "OK. I had not planned on wearing my tuxedo. David will return it for me."

Wanda said, "Great, I have your outfit in my car. I hope you like it."

Ben laughed and said, "I'm sure it's wonderful. You have a knack for dressing me."

Wanda smiled and said, "That's because you have a great body."

Ben smiled and said, "Oh, so you have checked out my body!"

Smiling Wanda said, "Yes, I have!"

Ben pulled her close and said, "I have checked out yours too and I like what I see!"

Wanda smiled and said, "I plan to get dressed at the Celebration Center."

Ben said, "I figured that. Mom has found a space for the guys too. We'll get dressed there too. It would be easier for David since he's catering."

Wanda kissed him lightly and said, "OK, only eight more days and we will be married."

Ben said, "I can't wait."

Finally, it was Friday before the wedding. Ben, Mr. Knowlton, Caleb, and David got their hair cut. The rehearsal was scheduled for six o'clock that evening. Everyone was in attendance. Wanda had three bridesmaids: Dee, Mary, and her college roommate, Ella. Ben had three groomsmen: David, Caleb, and Robert Knowlton, Wanda's uncle. There would be no flower girl or ring bearer. A trio from the church choir would sing.

The rehearsal went well, everyone understood their places. There was no official wedding planner since Wanda had planned everything. On the wedding day, Reverend Kings' wife, Mrs. Sophia, would direct everyone during the ceremony.

At the end of rehearsal, Reverend King said, "I'm so happy that you two are getting married. I remember when you were in middle school. That's when I came to New Providence Baptist Church."

Ben said, "That's right. I think I was in the sixth grade."

Reverend King said, "Yes, you were. Now, here you both are getting married."

Reverend King grimaced and touched his back.

Stepping closer Ben asked, "Are you OK?"

Reverend King said, "I'm fine. Today, I have been feeling this strange pain on my right side, but I'm sure it's fine."

Wanda said, "I hope so."

The rehearsal was over and everyone was departing the center.

Ben stood next to Wanda's car and said, "The next time I see you, you will be coming down the aisle."

Wanda said, "I know. Are you nervous?"

Ben said, "Not at all. I'm ready to be your husband."

Wanda said, "I'm not nervous either."

Ben kissed Wanda.

Wanda smiled and said, "I was hoping to get one of those long, passionate kisses."

Ben laughed and said, "No, I'm saving those for tomorrow."

On the next day Ben woke up early. He went for a run. He prayed while running and thanked God for everything. He thanked God for his health, his mind, the businesses, Wanda, his family, and friends. He asked God to take care of everything while he and Wanda were on their honeymoon.

It was finally time to go to the Celebration Center. He arrived at the center at eleven o'clock. He saw Wanda's car. He went to the dressing room. All the groomsmen were dressed by twelve noon, ahead of schedule. Mrs. King, the pastor's wife, knocked on the dressing room door.

Ben opened the door, smiled, and said, "Hi Mrs. King. I'm ready."

Mrs. King said, "Ben, I have some bad news. Reverend King is in the hospital. He won't be able to do your ceremony."

Ben asked, "Is he OK?"

Mrs. King said, "This morning he woke up in pain. We went to the emergency room around seven o'clock this morning. They immediately took him to surgery. He had to get his appendix taken out."

Ben asked, "How is he doing?"

Mrs. King said, "He is doing well. I have to get back to the hospital. I just wanted to let you know."

Ben said, "Thank you."

Mrs. King said, "All of the associate ministers are out of town this weekend."

Ben said surprisingly, "Oh!"

Mrs. King said, "I tried to call a pastor from one of the local churches, but none of them answered the phone this morning. I will keep trying, but it's almost too late."

Ben said, "OK! Thank you!"

Ben told the groomsmen what was going on. He was frantic. The ceremony was scheduled to start in one hour and they had no minister. Ben did not want to alarm Wanda. He jumped in his truck and took off. He drove to Mr. Jennings' house. Mr. Jennings was getting ready. While standing at the door, Ben told him his plight.

Mr. Jennings said, "Ben, my dad is a retired judge. Let me see if he will perform your ceremony."

Ben said, "That would be great."

Mr. Jennings said, "Come on in. He is eighty-three years old and he lives with me. It may take some time to get him dressed."

Ben followed Mr. Jennings into the house. Mr. Jennings' father was sitting in the Lazy Boy recliner. Mr. Jennings explained the problem. Mr. Jennings' father agreed to do the ceremony. His license was still valid. Mr. Jennings took his father to the bedroom to get him dressed. Ben tried to relax, but then he noticed in his haste that his white tuxedo had gotten a large smudge on it.

Ben exclaimed, "Oh, what have I done!"

Mrs. Jennings took him to the kitchen to clean it up. Surprisingly she was able to get it clean.

Mrs. Jennings said, "Ben, relax. Everything is going to be fine! Things happen and we have to solve the problem. We have solved two problems today. Hopefully, there won't be any more! Tonight, you and Wanda will laugh about this."

Trying to relax Ben said, "I hope so!"

Ben headed back to the center. He knew that the ceremony would not start on time, but at least they would have a ceremony. When he got to the center, Mary was waiting out front.

Mary said, "Where have you been? Wanda asked me if you were here. I had to tell her no. She is frantic."

Ben said, "I was here."

Mary said, "Ooh, you look very nice."

Ben said, "Thanks, so do you!"

Mary said, "You want me to tell Wanda something?"

Ben said, "No, I'll tell her."

Mary said, "You can't see her before she walks down the aisle."

Ben exclaimed, "I have to talk to her."

Thinking fast Mary said, "You can talk to her through the door, come with me!"

Mary went into the dressing room and told Wanda that Ben needed to talk to her. That she would crack the door so she could hear him.

Wanda said, "OK!"

Ben stood at the door and said, "Sweetheart, I'm sorry that you worried, but Mrs. King had to take Pastor King to the emergency room this morning. He had his appendix taken out. He's fine. Mrs. King tried to find a substitute minister but she was not able to."

Wanda exclaimed, "What!"

Ben said, "Everything is fine. I went over to Mr. Jennings' house to see if he could help. His father is a retired judge and his license is still valid. He agreed to marry us. The ceremony will not start on time, but as soon as he gets here we can start."

Wanda said, "Ben, thank you!"

Ben said, "I was frantic earlier too. I'm just glad it's all working out."

Wanda said, "When Mary did not see your truck, I knew something was wrong."

Ben said, "It was, but everything is back on track now. I will see you soon!"

Wanda stuck her hand out of the door, so that she could at least touch Ben.

Ben took her hand, kissed it ever so sweetly, and said, "I love you!"

Wanda said, "I love you more!"

Ben said, "I have to go and tell everyone else."

Guests were already arriving; the Celebration Center had started to fill up. Only two hundred people were invited to the wedding. One hundred of those people were from New Providence Baptist Church. The other hundred people included friends, distant family, college associates, and business colleagues.

Mom made an announcement that the ceremony would start late due to Pastor King being admitted into the hospital. She explained who would be officiating the ceremony. The trio sang songs to entertain the congregation. Finally, there was a knock on the door.

Ben opened the dressing room door and said, "Mr. Jennings, I'm so glad to see you."

Mr. Jennings said, "My dad is ready, we can start the ceremony. We did good, it's only 1:20 pm."

Ben laughed and said, "You saved the day. Thank you so much!"

Since Mrs. King was not there, Mom was able to get the neighbor, Miss Bessie, to act as coordinator and direct people down the aisle. The ceremony finally started and everything went smoothly. Judge Jennings wore his black robe. The big room was decorated beautifully. The wedding arch was decorated with blue and white flowers. Ben wore an all-white tuxedo with a royal blue bow tie and cummerbund. His groomsmen wore white jackets with black pants with matching tie and cummerbund. The boutonnieres were blue. They looked very nice.

The mothers wore royal blue dresses too. Mom looked very nice. Her dress was shorter than she normally wore her dresses. You could tell that she was a little self-conscious, she fidgeted. Ben smiled at her.

Mrs. Kennedy also wore a royal blue dress. Her dress was longer. The bride maids wore royal blue dresses with sweetheart necklines and short capped sleeves. The dresses were A-line and knee length. Their shoes were dyed the exact color of the dress. Their bouquets had white flowers and blue baby's breath. Wanda's roommate, Ella, came down the aisle first. When Mary walked down the aisle, Ben could see how much she had matured. She was a beautiful young lady. She looked like their mother. The last to come down the aisle was Dee. She looked older too. It seemed like only yesterday that they were pre-teens. Now, they were sixteen and seventeen years old. Mary would be going into her senior year, then going off to college.

When Dee walked down the aisle, Ben noticed that David was smiling. Dee had worn him down. He could tell that David liked her. The music changed, it was time for Wanda to walk down the aisle.

Wanda's dress was white with a sweetheart neckline with embroidered lace sleeves. It was a princess style dress with a two-foot train. Her veil was also embroidered with the same lace that was on her sleeves. You could see through the veil. She looked beautiful.

Ben stood at the altar taking it all in. He was so happy. He could not help thanking God for bringing him to this point. As Wanda walked down the aisle everyone stood up and oohed and awed. She looked beautiful.

Ben could not stop smiling. He was not nervous, he was happy. He had no regrets. Grandpa told him that God had a woman for him that would make him happier than he ever thought he could be. He was right.

Mr. William Knowlton, Wanda's father, escorted her down the aisle. Judge Jennings started the ceremony. He opened with a prayer and then said some very kind words. He thanked God for the opportunity to join this couple together. Finally, it was time for the exchange of vows. The couple had decided to each wear bands of gold. However, these bands had a distinctive floral pattern that went all around with a gold twisted rope on each side of the pattern. They were beautiful. The couple exchanged vows and rings.

Finally, Judge Jennings said, "You may now kiss your bride."

Ben stepped closer to Wanda, he was ready for this. Wanda looked at him with her beautiful, brown eyes and smiled. Ben leaned in and kissed his bride as lovingly as he could. He would save the passion for tonight. Today, he wanted her to know that he loved her.

When he finished Judge Jennings said, "I present to you Mr. & Mrs. Benjamin Davis."

Everyone stood up and applauded.

Ben walked his bride down the aisle, when they got to the foyer. He hugged her and kissed her again. Everyone was so happy. Pictures still needed to be taken. After the wedding party had left the room. Mom announced that pictures would be taken. She asked the guests to please be patient. This would only take about fifteen minutes.

The pictures took twenty minutes, but the guests entertained themselves and waited patiently. Some guests took out their cameras and took pictures too. Finally, it was time for the reception. The disc jockey played wonderful R&B listening music. A table was reserved for the bridal party. Ben and Wanda walked around to every table and thanked each guest for coming.

As they walked up to the table where Tammy's parents were seated, Ben said, "I am so glad that you could come. Mr. Kennedy, Mrs. Kennedy, this is my wife, Wanda. Wanda, these are Tammy's parents."

Wanda smiled and said, "I am so happy to meet you. Ben talks about you often."

Mrs. Kennedy said, "Wanda, you look beautiful. Ben, you look just as handsome as ever."

Wanda said, "Thank you so much."

Ben asked, "Is Paul here?"

Mr. Kennedy said, "Yes, he is. He went to the restroom. He told me to tell you that he has something for you."

Ben said, "Thanks. I will try to get back and talk to you all later."

Mrs. Kennedy said, "No problem, we understand. Enjoy yourself, you make a beautiful couple."

The next table is where Mr. Jennings, his wife, his father, Timothy Stevens and his wife were seated.

Mr. Jennings said, "It was a beautiful ceremony."

Mrs. Jennings said, "You both look wonderful. I haven't seen a happier couple."

Wanda said, "We are happy. I am glad that it shows."

Timothy Stevens said, "You both are glowing."

Mrs. Stevens said, "I am so glad that you invited us."

Ben said, "I am glad that you could come."

Wanda said, "Judge Jennings. thank you so much for saving the day."

Judge Jennings said, "Last year, I almost did not renew my license. I figured that I was eighty-three years old. I would not need it any more. I decided at the last minute to renew. I'm glad that I did."

Ben said, "We are too!"

Wanda motioned for the photographer to come over and take a picture of them. Wanda and Ben posed for a picture with the table. Wanda asked the photographer to try and get a picture of every table. She wanted to remember each of the guests. The photographer followed orders and took many pictures. The videographer tried to capture every moment. The last table was the family table. Wanda hugged her parents and Ben's mom.

Mr. William Knowlton said, "It was a beautiful ceremony."

Mrs. Knowlton said, "I was crying. I'm so glad I brought tissue."

Mom said, "It was a beautiful ceremony. I'm so happy for you."

Ben said, "Thank you Mom for everything."

Mom said, "Raising you has been my pleasure."

Ben hugged his mother tightly. Miss Bessie was standing nearby and motioned for the couple to have a seat at the bridal table. Ben and Wanda were glad to take a seat.

Wanda said, "I'm thirsty."

Ben said, "I am too!"

Next thing you know, Mary was walking toward them with a tray of glasses containing water and sweet tea. Ben took one of each for them both. The reception went along as planned. Robert Knowlton said grace. The bridal table was served and everyone else walked through the buffet line.

The food was delicious. David prepared chicken cordon bleu and flounder stuffed with crabmeat. Everyone talked about how good the food was. Ben and Wanda did not drink. So, no liquor was served at the reception.

David also baked the wedding cake. It was beautiful. It had three large tiers. Ben and Wanda cut the cake. More pictures were taken. A chair was placed on the dance floor, Ben removed her garter. Everyone oohed. Wanda tossed the bouquet to the single women. Miss Charlene caught it. Robert Knowlton smiled.

Finally, the dance floor was open for the couple's first dance. When they danced, you would have thought they were the only two people in the room. Ben did not want to let his new bride go. He realized that he should have picked a longer song.

The next dance was dedicated to mother and son, father and daughter. They danced around the room. Ben twirled his mother, she laughed out loud. It was a beautiful site.

Finally, the dance floor was open for all to dance. Everyone had a great time. Mary stayed on the dance floor. It seemed like all of the young men were asking her to dance. David took a break from the kitchen several times to dance with Dee. Ben looked up and he saw Tommy Savor at the back of the room. He excused himself from the table and went to talk to Tommy.

Tommy said, "I'm sorry that I'm late."

Ben smiled and said, "No problem, I was not worried."

Tommy said, "Here are the keys, the car is parked out front."

Ben hugged Tommy and said, "I really do appreciate it."

Tommy said, "Enjoy your honeymoon. I will see you when you get back."

Ben said, "Thanks!"

As he turned around he saw Paul.

Paul said, "Man, this was a beautiful wedding. I'm having a great time. The food is delicious. When does David graduate from culinary school?"

Ben said, "He has two more years."

Paul said, "He can quit now!"

Paul gave Ben a set of keys and said, "Here are your keys to the condo. I have stocked the refrigerator and pantry. The furniture you picked out has been delivered. The interior decorator has decorated it beautifully. It looks amazing."

Ben said, "I can't thank you enough!"

Paul said, "Call me in a couple of days, hopefully we all can have dinner."

Putting the keys in his pocket, Ben said, "I would like that!"

Paul hugged Ben and said, "I really am happy for you!"

Ben said, "Thanks!"

Ben danced with his wife several more times. Finally, it was time for them to go change clothes to leave. While they were changing, the ushers distributed small gifts and small bags of rice to everyone. Inside of the box was a two-inch by four-inch, beautiful crystal wedding bells with 'Ben & Wanda Davis July 7, 1979' engraved on them. All of the guests opened their gifts and oohed and awed.

Ben and Wanda rejoined the party. Wanda wore a beautiful knee length, white, laced dress with white sandals. Ben wore a white, short sleeve, linen shirt with navy blue slacks. They stood in front of the room.

Everyone applauded.

Ben said, "We are so glad all of you could share this special day with us. We are excited about our life together. As a token of our appreciation, the ushers have passed out small gifts of appreciation from us to you."

Wanda said, "We want to thank all of you who helped us organize this. We could not have done it without you."

Ben said, "Now, it is time for us to go!"

Ben took his wife's hand and led her out of the room. They were delayed by Miss Bessie, so the guests could exit first.

Caleb and Robert had put their luggage in the new car. The guests lined up to exit the room. Ben and Wanda tried to make their way through the crowd. They hugged, waved, and shook hands with so many people. When they finally made it outside, everyone was standing around the beautiful 1979 Malibu, oohing and awing. As Wanda and Ben walked toward the car, everyone threw rice.

Standing next to the car Wanda said, "Ben, you bought you a car!"

Ben said, "No, I bought you a car!"

Wanda hugged Ben and exclaimed, "I love it. I love you Ben. You think of everything."

Ben said, "I'm trying to."

Ben opened the passenger door for his bride to get in. He waved goodbye to David and Mary, then hugged his mother one last time before he got in the car.

Everyone watched and waved as they drove away.

10

THE HONEYMOON

July 7, 1979 was a beautiful summer day in Fairville, Georgia. It was approximately 4:15 pm as they drove away from the Cason's Celebration Center. In the rearview mirror Ben could see all of his family and loved ones waving goodbye. It was bittersweet. He looked at his beautiful bride sitting next to him and grabbed her hand.

Wanda said, "Ben, I love you very much!"

Ben said, "I love you too."

Wanda said, "It was a beautiful ceremony."

Ben said, "Yes, it was. I can't believe that an hour before, we didn't have a minister."

Wanda said, "I knew something was wrong when Mary didn't see your truck. I started to pray. I asked God to fix whatever was wrong. I was trying not to cry, but I was very worried."

Ben said, "Well, God heard your prayer. When I realized that we needed help, I jumped in my truck and took off. At first, I didn't know where I was going, but then God dropped the thought of Mr. Jennings in my head. So, I went to his house. You know the rest."

Wanda said, "I didn't want anything to stop our wedding today."

Ben said, "While I was at Mr. Jennings' house, I noticed that I had messed up my white tuxedo."

Wanda smiled and looked confused.

Ben said, "Mrs. Jennings cleaned it up for me."

Wanda said, "I didn't see any marks. All I saw was my handsome fiancé standing at the altar waiting for me. You looked extremely nice today. Not that you are not handsome every day, but you looked really good in that tuxedo. You also smell very nice. I really like that cologne."

Ben said, "I'm glad. I'm sure everyone told you how beautiful you looked today. You really are beautiful. I loved the wedding dress you selected. When I first saw you at the back of the room, my heart stopped. As you moved closer, my heart started to beat faster. I had to calm myself down. I realized this beautiful woman was in love with me and agreed to marry me. I did not cry, but I did get choked up."

Wanda said, "I'm so thankful that God put us together. Sometimes it feels like a dream."

Ben said, "I know. I feel the same way!"

Wanda said, "Ben, I still can't believe you bought me this car."

Ben asked, "Do you like it?"

Wanda exclaimed, "What's not to like? It has leather seats, air conditioning, cassette, and the interior is not black!"

Ben said, "I know you like to pick things out for yourself, but you needed a reliable vehicle. Grandpa told me there comes a time when you have to make a decision whether to continue fixing a car or get another one."

Wanda smiled and said, "You're right. We already fixed my car at least two times in the last three months."

Ben said, "Yes! We could not go on our honeymoon in the truck. All of our luggage could get wet!"

Wanda laughed and said, "That's true. You're always thinking about what's best for us."

Ben said, "I try."

Wanda leaned into Ben and laid her head on his right shoulder, then she said, "OK, now that we're married. Where are we going on our honeymoon?"

Ben laughed and said, "OK, I have given this a lot of thought. I didn't want our first night to be filled with travel. If we flew somewhere, we would have to drive to Atlanta, catch a flight and then possibly catch a connecting flight to our destination."

Wanda said, "I would not have liked that!"

Ben said, "I did not like that idea either. So, our final destination will be Atlanta. If you want, we can spend the night in Macon, which you know is an hour and a half away or we can drive all the way to Atlanta which is two and a half hours away."

Wanda said, "I would rather drive all the way to Atlanta. Once I get you in the hotel room, I may not be ready to leave tomorrow morning."

Ben laughed and said, "I was thinking the same thing. So, we are driving to Atlanta!"

Wanda said, "I don't mind the drive. I'm with the man that I love, so I'm fine."

Ben said, "Good. Oh! I forgot something!"

Wanda asked, "What did you forget?"

Ben said, "Well, I figured we could listen to my cassettes on the trip. I left them in my truck."

Wanda said, "No problem. We can just listen to the radio."

Wanda programmed the radio to their favorite R&B station in Macon. They talked and laughed the entire trip. They stopped to get ice cream at Dairy Queen. During the stop they were able to see the 'just married' sign on the back of the car. They laughed, Wanda took a picture. The two and a half hours went by fast. Finally, they were in the big city of Atlanta. It was about 7:30 pm.

Ben asked, "Are you hungry?"

Wanda said, "Not really. Are you?"

Ben said, "No, I'm fine. During the reception, I ate both the chicken cordon bleu and the stuffed flounder. They were delicious."

Wanda said, "The food was delicious. David is a great chef."

Ben said, "Yes, he is. I'm very proud of him."

Wanda smiled and said, "Dee's crush is getting bigger and bigger."

Ben said, "I think David is starting to like her too!"

Wanda said, "That's good!"

Looking out the car window, Wanda asked, "How much further before we get there? What's the name of the hotel, I'll help you look for it."

Ben said, "We're about five minutes away. I want this to be a surprise."

Ben pulled a blind fold out of his pocket and gave it to Wanda.

Ben said, "I don't want you to see the place until we're at the door."

Holding the blind fold in the air Wanda asked, "You want me to put on this blind fold?"

Ben said lovingly, "I really do."

Wanda said sweetly, "You don't have to surprise me anymore."

Ben said, "I really want to."

Wanda said, "OK. You know I'm not a fan of blind folds. I like to see what's coming."

Ben said, "I know, just trust me."

Wanda smiled and said, "You know I do."

Ben said, "I will let you know when to put the blind fold on. We have about three more minutes."

Wanda said, "OK! Ben, I'm sure that I will love this surprise. Thanks for going through so much trouble for me."

Ben said, "I love you. My goal is to not only make you happy, but for you to never regret marrying me."

Wanda said, "I can't imagine ever regretting that. This is the best decision I ever made."

Ben laughed and said, "OK, please put on the blind fold and no peeking."

Wanda said, "I won't peek."

Wanda felt the car slowing down and turning right. The car slowed down, but it never stopped.

Ben said, "We're almost there. I'm just looking for a parking space."

Wanda said, "OK!"

He stopped the car.

Ben said, "I'm just getting out of the car to come open your door."

Wanda laughed and said, "Thanks for the play by play!"

Ben said, "I will come back down stairs to get our luggage."

Wanda said, "OK!"

Ben took her hand and led her to the elevator.

Ben said, "We're going to the fifth floor."

Wanda asked, "You already checked into the hotel?"

Ben said, "Quit trying to figure it out. Just relax."

Wanda laughed.

The elevator stopped on the fifth floor. Ben took Wanda's hand and led her to the door. He unlocked the front door and opened it. Then he gently removed her blind fold and kissed her.

Wanda exclaimed, "I love your kisses."

Ben picked her up in his arms and carried her across the threshold.

Wanda put her arms around Ben's neck and said, "I like this too."

Ben said, "You aren't heavy!"

Wanda said, "Good, I always wanted a strong man that could pick me up!"

Ben laughed and said, "Even if you weighed more, I will always be there to pick you up."

Wanda laughed.

Once inside the condominium, Wanda looked around and said, "Ben, this is not a hotel room!"

Ben said, "No, it's not. Remember, Paul works with real estate part-time. He hooked me up and we are spending our honeymoon here in this condo. I thought it may get cramped in the hotel room after a while."

Wanda exclaimed, "This is very nice, so beautifully decorated. I love the furniture. This place is very big."

Ben agreed, "Yes, it's a little big."

Wanda hugged Ben and said, "I love it!"

Ben said, "Great. I'm just going to run down stairs and get our luggage."

Ben kissed her very sweetly. She pulled him back and kissed him very passionately.

Ben exclaimed, "OK, Wanda! I'm trying to go down stairs. I could leave the luggage in the car if you want."

Wanda laughed.

While Ben was gone to get the luggage. Wanda toured the beautiful, spacious condo. She opened the refrigerator, looked in the pantry, and opened the cabinets and drawers. She walked through each of the three bedrooms. Both of the smaller bedrooms were decorated just as nice as the rest of the condo.

The balcony had a patio table and two chairs. There were two bathrooms. The master bedroom was luxurious. She oohed and awed. When she walked into the master bath, she found a shower big enough for two people and a separate jacuzzi bath tub. There were two sinks and two very large mirrors. She heard the door open and ran back to the living room.

Wanda exclaimed, "Ben, this place is wonderful! It's palatial."

Ben smiled and said, "I'm glad you like it."

Wanda said, "The refrigerator is stocked with all of our favorite foods. The pantry is also stocked. Everything we need is in that kitchen."

Ben said, "Great, Paul went shopping for us."

Wanda said, "I am in awe."

Ben pulled her close and said, "I'm glad that you like it. I wanted us to be comfortable."

Twirling around Wanda exclaimed, "I'm very comfortable!"

Ben said, "I'm thirsty!"

Wanda asked, "What would you like? Everything is in the refrigerator."

Ben said, "A coke would be great."

Wanda retrieved a coke for Ben with a glass of ice. Ben sat at the table and drank his coke.

Wanda said, "Ben, I'm speechless. I know that we can't live like this all the time. However, I'm happy to live like this for our honeymoon."

Ben laughed and asked, "How long do you want to stay?"

Wanda said, "I would love to stay here more than one week."

Ben said, "I was thinking we could stay for at least two weeks. If you want to stay longer we can. Uncle Robert said he could take care of the store and for us not to rush back."

Wanda said, "Let's stay for at least two weeks and we can decide if we want to stay longer after that."

Ben smiled and said, "No problem. Paul said that we can stay as long as we like."

Wanda hugged Ben and said, "Please don't give me any more surprises. I have had enough today to last me for a very long time."

Ben laughed.

Wanda said, "I need to take a shower. It's been a long day!"

Drinking the last of his coke, Ben said, "OK, I'll let you go first."

Wanda said, "I was thinking we could take one together. The shower is big enough for two!"

Ben smiled and said, "I like the way you think!"

After a beautiful night of consummating their marriage, Wanda got up early. She sat on the balcony and prayed. She thanked God for all that he was doing in their lives. She asked God to help her be the best wife she could be for Ben. She thanked God for everything that he had done for them. As she was praying, Ben walked onto the balcony.

Ben said, "Good morning sweetheart! I didn't mean to sleep so late!"

Wanda said, "That's fine. I needed some time to pray!"

Ben hugged her and asked, "Do you need some more time?"

Wanda said, "No, I'm finished. This view is beautiful. I love it!"

Ben reached to hug his wife and said, "I really enjoyed last night."

Wanda said, "I did too. I'm glad we waited for each other to be our first. Last night was amazing and very memorable."

Ben said, "I am too. You were definitely worth the wait."

Wanda said, "I hope you have enough energy for this morning."

Ben said, "I'm glad we started running. It has helped my endurance!"

Wanda smiled and said, "Yes, it has. I will take it easy on you this morning."

Ben laughed and said, "Please, don't take it easy on me!"

Wanda laughed.

Ben said, "Before we go back to bed. I really have something I need to tell you."

Wanda said, "OK!"

Ben said, "Let's step inside."

When Wanda stepped inside, there was a box of Kleenex, a glass of water, and a coke on the coffee table. Wanda saw the things on the table and looked at Ben confused.

Ben said, "Please have a seat. What I have to tell you is not bad news. It's just something that I have to say."

Wanda relaxed and took a seat on the sofa.

Ben said, "I know that you don't like surprises."

Wanda said, "Normally, I don't like surprises, but your surprises have all been great. So, I'm not against surprises, as much as I used to be."

Ben smiled and said, "I'm glad. You know how much I

love you! You know that I plan to work hard to provide for you and our family."

Wanda said, "I know, I'm not worried about that. We're both capable of working hard. I believe we can do great things with the sporting goods store and it will provide us a great living."

Ben smiled and said, "I do too. I have some things I have to tell you that I could not say before we were married."

Wanda said, "Well, you said it was not bad news. So, I'm OK. Please say what you need to say."

Ben said, "You remember I told you about the things that had been saved for me and how they changed my life."

Wanda said, "Yes, the job at the golf shop and your first truck."

Ben said, "Yes, that's true. There were a few other things that have been saved for me. I found out about them when Grandpa died."

Wanda said, "You said that he left you his golf shop and the large building next door that you renovated for the new store. Then you found out about the event center."

Ben said, "That's correct, but there were a few other things too. Remember, I could not tell you about them until today."

Wanda shifted her weight and said, "OK!"

Ben said, "When Mr. Jennings initially told me this information, he broke it down into three categories. I'll do the same for you."

Wanda saw that Ben was fidgeting, she said, "Ben, don't be nervous. You know you can tell me anything. Why are you nervous?"

Ben said, "I'm nervous because, I don't want you to get upset that I did not tell you before."

Wanda said, "Oh! I know when we had our first argument,

I told you that I don't like to be deceived. I don't think you're deceiving me. You just couldn't share with me before today."

Ben smiled and said, "That's exactly right! I feel much better. OK, the first category is residential property. Grandpa left me about twelve pieces of residential property that are currently being rented in Fairville. A realty company in Macon manages all of those properties. No one knew that Grandpa owned the properties. He established a parent company that those properties fall under."

Smiling Wanda said, "That's great. Residential rental property is a great investment."

Ben said, "Yes, it is. The second group falls under commercial property. Grandpa left me some other commercial property that is currently rented to businesses. The Maxwell store, Rexall Drug Store, Dime Store, the laundry mat, the dry cleaners, and the old movie theater. He gave the old city café to David."

Sitting up straight Wanda asked, "Are you saying that you own that property too?"

Ben said, "Yes, we own that property too. The last group of property is industrial property. Grandpa owned the textile factory on the north side of town. He did not own the company; the company just leases the factory from him. They pay a substantial amount each month to lease that property."

Wanda took a sip of water and said, "OK, Ben that's a lot of property. You're saying no one knew he owned all of this!"

Ben said, "That's correct. Mr. Jennings suggests that no one should know that we own it either. It's for our protection. So, we can live a normal life in Fairville."

Wanda adjusted her hips and took another sip of water and said, "I understand that."

Ben said, "That's all of the property. There are several

shares of stocks that he left me. He left me IBM, Honeywell, Trane, and a few others. Those stocks have done very well."

Wanda stood up, then sat back down, and said, "So, you're saying we own stocks in those premier companies too."

Ben said, "Yes, that's true. There are also several bank accounts. Grandpa set up various accounts for different reasons. Those accounts have substantial amounts of money in them."

As her mind raced, Wanda asked, "Are you saying your grandfather was a millionaire?"

Ben said, "Yes, he was worth approximately thirty-five million dollars."

Placing her left hand on her head, Wanda stood up again and said, "So, you're telling me that you're worth thirty-five million dollars."

Ben said, "No, I'm saying we are worth about forty-five million dollars. You remember the bowling alley, new movie theater, and Putt-Putt golf course that were built recently. Those were my ideas, so with the new sporting goods store and the event center. We're now worth about forty-five million dollars."

Wanda walked around the room, then she asked, "Ben, are you serious?"

Ben walked closer to his wife and said, "Yes!"

Wanda's knees went weak. Ben caught her in his arms, He asked, "Are you OK?"

Getting her balance, Wanda said, "Ben, this is hard to believe. I never doubted that you would be able to provide for our family. This is too much to believe."

Ben said, "I know. When Mr. Jennings first told me, I was overwhelmed."

Wanda exclaimed, "It is overwhelming!"

Ben said, "Oh, here are some checks for our personal account and a couple of credit cards for you."

Looking at the credit cards Wanda exclaimed, "Ben, this is an American Express Black card!"

Ben said, "Yes, it is."

Wanda asked, "How much money is in our personal account?"

Ben said, "Approximately two hundred and fifty thousand dollars!"

Wanda exclaimed, "Two hundred and fifty thousand dollars!"

Then she sat back down again.

Ben said, "That's after I transferred the money to your account for the wedding and graduation dinner. I also withdrew some cash for the honeymoon!"

With tears rolling down her cheeks Wanda exclaimed, "Ben!"

Ben said, "I know what you're thinking. Oh, there's one thing I forgot to tell you."

Wiping her tears with the Kleenex and drinking more water Wanda said, "Please don't tell me anything else. I can't take it."

Ben said, "I'll save the rest for later, but I have to tell you this."

Wanda drank some of the coke this time and said, "OK, I'm ready."

Ben said, "This beautiful condo that you love so much, it's ours."

Wanda jumped up and exclaimed, "This place is ours!"

Ben said, "Yes, I bought it last month for our honeymoon. I thought it was a great investment. Since Atlanta was two and a half hours away, when we need to get away from Fairville, we would have somewhere to go."

Pacing back and forth with the tissue in her hand, Wanda said, "Ben, I can't believe this. It's going to take me a little while to adapt to this information."

Ben said, "It took me a little while too."

Wanda asked, "Did you say that you have grown that thirty-five million dollars to forty-five million dollars in just one year?"

Ben said, "Yes, I have."

Wanda stepped closer to Ben and said, "You're a great businessman. I love you!"

Ben asked, "So, you're not mad at me for not telling you earlier?"

Wanda said, "Of course not, I'm glad that you didn't tell me earlier. I would not want you to think that I married you for your money."

Ben said, "For our safety, no one can know exactly what we own. Right now, we can only talk to others about the store and the event center."

Wanda said, "No problem. Nobody would believe it anyway!"

Wanda twirled around the room, Ben smiled.

Ben exclaimed, "That's the same thing I said!"

Wanda said, "So your family doesn't know any of this."

Ben said, "That's correct. All they know about is the store, the event center, and Grandpa's house."

Wanda said, "When we went to the grand opening of the movie theater, I should have known something was up. You didn't act like you were seeing it for the first time."

Ben smiled and said, "Oh! I have to improve my acting skills. You're right. I approved the plans. I also walked through it when it was being built and before the grand opening."

Wanda laughed.

Ben said, "I won't tell you anything else about our finances now, but there are a few other things you need to know."

Wanda said, "Please don't tell me anything else right now. It's going to take me a while to digest all of this. I'm in love with a millionaire!"

Ben said, "And he loves you more than he ever thought he could."

Wanda asked, "Why didn't you ask me to sign a pre-nup?"

Ben said, "I would not have married you, if I thought I could not share all that I have with you. We're going to be married for a very long time."

Wanda said, "Yes we are. God put us together and I'm not letting you go!"

Ben walked closer to Wanda and took her hand.

Ben said, "All of these things that God saved for me are truly wonderful, but there is one thing that I'm the most thankful for."

Wanda asked, "What's that?"

Looking straight into her beautiful, brown eyes Ben said, "He saved you for me."

Wanda hugged him. Ben picked up his beautiful wife and carried her to the bedroom.

Later that afternoon, Ben was sitting on the balcony.

Wanda opened the door and said, "I can't believe I took that long of a nap."

Ben laughed and said, "You needed to recharge. You expended all of your energy earlier."

Wanda smiled and exclaimed, "Yes I did!"

Ben asked, "Would you like to eat in or go out to dinner?"

Wanda said, "I want to eat in. I'm not ready to share you with anyone yet."

Ben laughed and said, "In a few days, Paul would like to have dinner with us."

Wanda said, "That will be fun!"

Ben said, "I called Mom and your parents to let them know that we're fine."

Wanda asked, "Thanks! Will we ever be able to let anyone know that we own this condo?"

Ben said, "Yes, I think we can share that. We make enough money at the store to have purchased it."

Wanda said, "Great. These extra bedrooms will come in handy when David graduates from culinary school."

Ben said, "I know. Now, if there's anything that you want to change in here, we can. I picked out the furniture. If you don't like it, my feelings won't be hurt."

Wanda said, "Truthfully, I really like it. You did a great job. You have a great eye."

Ben laughed and said, "Now remember, I had an interior decorator to help me!"

Wanda asked, "When we go back to Fairville, have you thought about where we will live?"

Ben said, "Yes, I have. In that residential property that we own, there's Grandpa's house. Mr. Jennings is getting it spruced up for us. I did purchase a bedroom set and a dinette set before I left. I figured you would want to decorate the rest of the house."

Wanda laughed and said, "You're right! We will need a bed and a place to eat immediately. That's great."

Ben said, "Grandpa told me that some of his neighbors were prejudice. So, we don't have to stay there long, we can build something if you want."

Wanda said, "No, I want to stay there. If we need to keep a low profile, we don't need to build a house just yet."

Ben smiled and said, "Good idea! Mr. Jennings said that one of the neighbors that was very prejudice died. There is one sixty-five-year-old widow, Agnes Boatwright, that still lives right across the street. He said that she could be adversarial and surly."

Wanda said, "I have no disdain concerning Mrs. Boatwright. God has given us all of this, he will take care of her."

Ben said, "I agree."

Wanda said, "I think we need to include all of our neighbors in our prayers."

Ben said, "Great idea."

Over the next three weeks, Ben and Wanda had a great time. They shopped and hung out with Paul a few times. They spent time with Caleb. They attended Broadway plays. They went to museums and amusement parks. They lounged around the condo, swam in the pool, and watched movies. Finally, they made the decision to go back to Fairville. It was hard to say goodbye to the condo, but they were ready.

On the drive back to Fairville, Wanda said, "Ben, that honeymoon was above and beyond what I thought it would be."

Ben said, "I had a great time too."

Wanda asked, "Did you make the anonymous donation to the church?"

Ben said, "Yes, I did."

Wanda smiled and said, "I'm glad that it was you."

Ben said, "You know the new structure on Highway 137."

Wanda said, "Yes, it doesn't have a sign yet, but it looks like storage units."

Ben said, "That's correct. It belongs to us too."

Wanda said, "You have been very busy."

Ben said, "Yes, I have been working hard. I'm glad that you can help me from now on."

Wanda said, "I look forward to it."

Ben said, "Oh, also on Highway 137, there will be a self-service car wash."

Wanda said, "That's a great idea. It does not require a lot of management and it's a money maker."

Ben laughed and said, "We're more alike than you know."

Wanda smiled.

Ben said, "We're almost home. This is the street."

Ben parked the car in the driveway. The house looked brand new. The brick had been power washed, the shutters and trim had been painted, the lawn had been cut, and flowers were blooming in the flower beds. Ben opened Wanda's car door.

Wanda exclaimed, "This is a very nice house."

Ben said, "It looks great. Mr. Jennings really did spruce it up."

Ben lifted up the new welcome mat and found the key. He unlocked the door. Wanda tried to go in. Ben gently pulled her back.

Ben said, "I have to carry you across the threshold again. This is our house; I want to do it again!"

Wanda laughed and asked, "You're such a gentleman! Who am I to argue with your logic?"

When they got in the house, it was beautiful. The walls were painted pale blue throughout. Even though there was no furniture in the living room. It looked great. New carpet had been installed. All of the wedding gifts were neatly stacked next to the wall. The dinette set that Ben selected was very nice. New curtains had been hung. When they walked into the master bedroom, it was gorgeous. Ben had picked out a queen size bedroom set. The furniture was high quality wood, very nice.

Wanda asked, "Ben, did you select this furniture?"

Ben replied, "Yes, but this time I didn't have an interior decorator. So, if you don't like it, that's OK."

Wanda said, "I love it. I really like that headboard. The bedspread is beautiful. I like everything. I think we'll be very happy here."

Ben smiled and said, "I know we will."

Wanda toured the kitchen. A new refrigerator, stove, and dishwasher had been installed. The kitchen cabinets had been resurfaced and painted. The refrigerator was stocked and there was food in the pantry. In the laundry room she found a new washer and dryer. The floors had been waxed and all of the windows had been cleaned. The house looked brand new.

Wanda said, "Mr. Jennings did a great job. We need to send him a very special thank you card."

In awe Ben said, "I'm sure his wife made suggestions, but this is very nice."

Wanda said, "It's not the condo, but I really do like it."

Ben pulled her close and said, "I do too!"

Wanda said, "I think we should go ahead and pray over our house."

Ben said, "Great idea."

They held hands and Ben prayed, "Thank you God for the beautiful and spacious home that you had provided. Please soften the hearts of the neighbors to accept us for who we are and not reject us based on the color of our skin. God help us to be the light that the neighborhood needs and help us be good stewards over all you have blessed us with. In Jesus name we pray! Amen!"

Wanda said, "Amen! That was a beautiful prayer."

Ben kissed his wife on the forehead and said, "Thanks, I will unload the car."

Wanda busied herself in the house, preparing herself for what God had in store for them.

As Ben unloaded the car, he reflected on all that had happened in the last year. He trusted his omnipotent God and asked him to prepare them for what was to come!

To be continued…

Continue on this amazing journey with Ben as he discovers all that God has saved for him. Order today:

Book 1 Saved for Ben   ISBN 978-1-6642-6888-3
Book 2 Saved for Ben: The College Years ISBN 978-1-6642-6892-0
Book 3 Saved for Ben: Ben and Wanda   ISBN 978-1-6642-6895-1
Book 4 Saved for Ben: The Legacy   ISBN 978-1-6642-6898-2

Stay tuned for the continuing saga!

Printed in the United States
by Baker & Taylor Publisher Services